THE
BLOODIED IVY

Other Nero Wolfe books by Robert Goldsborough

Murder in E Minor

Death on Deadline

· *A NERO WOLFE MYSTERY* ·

THE
BLOODIED IVY

Robert Goldsborough

BANTAM BOOKS

TORONTO · NEW YORK · LONDON · SYDNEY · AUCKLAND

THE BLOODIED IVY
A Bantam Book / August 1988

Library of Congress Cataloging-in-Publication Data

Goldsborough, Robert.
    The bloodied ivy.

    I. Title.
PS3557.03849B56   1988   813'.54   88-3513
ISBN 0-553-05281-0

Published simultaneously in the United States and Canada

Bantam Books are published by Bantam Books, a division of Bantam Doubleday Dell Publishing
Group, Inc. Its trademark, consisting of the words "Bantam Books" and the portrayal of a rooster,
is Registered in U.S. Patent and Trademark Office and in other countries. Marca Registrada.
Bantam Books, 666 Fifth Avenue, New York, New York 10103.

PRINTED IN THE UNITED STATES OF AMERICA
DH   0 9 8 7 6 5 4 3 2 1

FOR SUZY, BOB, COLLEEN, AND BONNIE

INTRODUCTION

Recently, someone asked me what it was like to be Rex Stout's daughter. I've learned to interpret the familiar gleam I noticed in the eye of the questioner. She was *really* saying, "Come on, tell me the real story, the juicy stuff." I was sorry to disappoint her, and I finally had to admit that the Stout family has no closetful of titillating secrets. In fact, the world as I knew it when I was growing up was satisfying, interesting—and most remarkable for its ordinariness.

My family lived in Manhattan for a few years, but most of my childhood was spent at High Meadow, my parents' sprawling haven on the New York-Connecticut border, about fifty miles north of New York City. The U-shaped house, designed and built by my father, the gardens, the orchards, and the acres of rolling hills provided the setting for our daily lives. The High Meadow years were quiet, happy, and filled with experiences that countless other American children would recognize.

I enjoyed school, although, like any child, I looked forward to the end of day so that I could run down the street to find my father and his car. Since we lived too far from Danbury for me to walk to school as most of the other children did, Dad would come many afternoons to pick me up in the chocolate-colored Cadillac that would be the family automobile for nearly twenty years. One blustery autumn day, a third-grade friend caught up with me as I was running down the street toward the Cadillac.

She tugged at my sleeve and whispered in my ear, "What's it like to have *him* for a father?"

Well, that stopped me for a moment; I thought about her question. My first notion was that I liked it when Dad helped me with my homework. He checked on my progress and encouraged me, but he never gave me the answers, making sure, instead, that I knew how to arrive at the solutions myself. Then I thought about bedtime, when he'd come upstairs, grab my sister Barbara and me in his arms, and sing "Good Night, Ladies" and then toss us gleefully onto our beds.

Still, at age eight, I wasn't quite sure what there was about my father that would be quite so impressive to a classmate. I smiled and told her that having him for a father was fine.

"Only fine?" she asked, her face scrunching into a skeptical frown as she eyed the white beard resting on his chest. "Don't you think it's *terrific* to have Santa Claus for a father?"

That was my first inkling that Dad was notable.

It was about that time in my life that I began to wonder what my father did for a living. It wasn't a worry—just a curiosity that came and went at idle moments. After all, other fathers went off with briefcases on the commuter trains, or worked at farms or stores. What I did know was that several times a year a scenario was repeated that started with my father moving through the house and puttering in the gardens without really hearing what anyone said to him. He'd become vague and distracted, and Barbara and I soon learned to talk to him only when it was necessary during those periods. As I grew older, I realized that he was working—getting to know his characters, setting out the story—before he moved into his writing routine.

Then, when he began the actual writing, Dad would disappear into his study precisely at noon and reappear for dinner promptly at six-thirty. Even when we couldn't hear the old manual typewriter clattering away, my sister and I weren't allowed to play in the court beneath his window during those hours. In fact, loud conversation in the kitchen would evoke admonitions from above to be quiet. This would go on for a couple of weeks, occasionally for as long as two months, and then, his book or story complete, he'd be done for a while.

Later in my life, when I learned that my father never rewrote anything and that his books were published exactly as he first set the words down, I was more than a little amazed—but for years I assumed that everyone else who wrote fiction worked in the same way.

He brought the same high standards to other tasks. In addition to his writing, Dad was an avid gardener and an enthusiastic carpenter. He spent long hours making furniture that he designed himself, using old-fashioned doweled construction to build pieces that are marvels of craftsmanship. His dresser drawers still, after thirty years, slide without sticking on the runners; whatever he made seems to stand up to the tests of time.

His shop was always filled with boxes of fragrant scrap wood, which delighted me when I was a child. Under his tutelage, I began my carpentry lessons by learning to wield a hammer, and eventually graduated to the use of his electric saw—the same machine that claimed a part of one of his fingers when he became distracted while using it.

For all his involvement with writing, gardening, and carpentry, Dad thrived on contact with people. Even when he was working on a book, he had regular conferences with Harold Salmon, who worked at High Meadow taking care of the grounds and generally seeing to maintenance. As a young child, I thought of Harold more as a part of the family than as an employee. Then, after World War II, my parents sponsored the Yasamotos, a Japanese-American family who came to stay with us at High Meadow after they'd lived in the internment camps. They became an integral part of our household, sharing dinner, joining in the nightly game of Twenty Questions, and enlarging our family once again.

My mother, during this period, made a name for herself in a separate arena. She designed and eventually manufactured her own fabrics; Dad encouraged her enterprising independence. For a time my mother even endured the long commute from Brewster, New York, to

Philadelphia, to her mill. She, too, was nourished by her creativity and was particularly proud of her wools. When the Philadelphia Museum announced that Mother would be given an award to honor her textile designs, Dad decided that we should all attend in clothing made of her fabrics. I can still remember the beautiful green wool dress I wore; Dad, too, stood up proudly in his wool suit. The fact that the ceremony was held on a sweltering, humid midsummer Philadelphia day was of little consequence in Dad's choice of wardrobe—he was determined that we would all show off Mother's handiwork!

When he wasn't planning or writing his next tale, the house was often filled with visitors. Marian Anderson, Mark Van Doren, Kip Fadiman, my aunt Ruth Stout, and countless others would come to High Meadow to share the conversation, laughter, food, and drink. Barbara and I, indeed, any children who happened to be around, were always treated as social equals in a group. We listened, we joined the discussions, and we had a grand time.

Dad particularly loved barbecues, and a series of traditional gatherings at High Meadow, starting with the blooming of the first iris each spring, would find him at the huge stone fireplace under the trees. He presided like a monarch over the wood fire, anointing the chickens with his homemade sauce dripping from his special baster: a long dowel to which he'd attached chicken feathers at one end. Memorial Day, Fourth of July (my sister and I were always decked out in red, white, and blue), and Labor Day, whatever the progress of his latest book or story, Rex Stout became chef for the occasion and grilled chickens, two-inch-thick steaks, corn, and potatoes: a feast to feed his hungry friends.

Despite—or perhaps because of—the comings and goings of such famous people in my life, it wasn't until I was a high school sophomore at Oakwood, a Quaker prep school in Poughkeepsie, New York, that I really became aware of my father's celebrity status. I was on my own, and for the first time I sensed the ways in which my childhood truly was different from many of my classmates. I developed a friendship with Gail Jones, Lena Horne's daughter. Without understanding the initial reasons for our unspoken bond, we later recognized the common experiences we shared as the offspring of famous parents.

Never at a loss for something to say about the world in which he lived, it's not surprising that my father had strong opinions about education. He felt that everyone should be well grounded in the basics of reading, writing, and mathematics, but he didn't place special value on higher education, although he never discouraged my sister and me from attending college. Dad never went to college himself, but he didn't consider that a disadvantage. An educated person, he liked to say, is one who has the capacity to distinguish the important from the unimportant, has the ability to recognize good literature, has acquired sufficient knowledge of history to make connections between the past and the present, and can sustain a curiosity about the world and a desire to continue learning. Certainly, by those criteria, he was summa cum laude.

I can hardly remember an instance when my father raised his voice in anger or to make a point. Instead, an eyebrow would shoot up and he'd say very evenly, "Do you think that's a good idea?" The message was unmistakable—*he* didn't think it was good idea. But part of the lesson was to figure out just why he didn't like the idea and then come up with an acceptable alternative. He seldom told my sister and me what to do; in fact, he rarely even gave advice. We learned early on that if we wanted his opinion, we'd have to ask, "What would you do, Dad?" When we did, his responses very often centered around the concepts of fairness, reasonableness, and consistency.

If I was confused about what I saw in the world, he'd wait until I expressed a specific concern, giving me the opportunity to work things out without intervention if I could. I recall wrestling during my adolescence with the feeling that it wasn't fair for some people to have great material comforts when others didn't. When I finally told him what was bothering me, my father counseled, "There's no need to feel guilty about what you have as long as you've worked for it and you share it with others. Everyone has different opportunities; it's what you do with the opportunities you have that counts."

Out of such moments, I began to understand what was important to my father. As an adult, I realize that most of what I've learned from him was communicated not so much in his words as through the example of his life.

He placed enormous value on honesty. (I never even considered lying to him. Whatever the consequences of telling the truth, they were easier to live with than his reactions to a lie.) Organization and responsibility were traits high on his list. (He never complained about paying taxes and always paid all his bills as soon as they arrived. This habit has been so persistent with me that I've managed to pass it on to my own children without even once telling them that it was something they should do.) He taught me about generosity by demonstrating how much joy comes to the giver. He never attached strings to his gifts—even though the recipient might want to imagine some. He never held a grudge. He hated phonies utterly. He believed that the writer's job is to tell a good story and to comment on human behavior, because above all, Dad valued people.

Of the qualities that made my father unique, the most memorable was the quiet intensity he brought to everything he did. He worked, played, and fought for what he believed with a passion. He loved writing; the zest he brought to that task enlivens the pages of his books. I have the feeling that Robert Goldsborough probably has experienced some of the same delight that showed on Dad's face when, after his alloted six and a half hours at the typewriter, he emerged from his upstairs study, slid into his chair at the dinner table, and announced with a twinkle, "You won't believe what Archie just said to Wolfe!"

Rebecca Stout Bradbury
La Jolla, California
February, 1988

ONE

Hale Markham's death had been big news, of course. It was even the subject of a brief conversation I had with Nero Wolfe. We were sitting in the office, he with beer and I with a Scotch-and-water, going through our copies of the *Gazette* before dinner.

"See where this guy up at Prescott U. fell into a ravine on the campus and got himself killed?" I asked, to be chatty. Wolfe only grunted, but I've never been one to let a low-grade grunt stop me. "Wasn't he the one whose book—they mention it here in the story: *Bleeding Hearts Can Kill*—got you so worked up a couple of years back?"

Wolfe lowered his paper, sighed, and glared at a spot on the wall six inches above my head. "The man was a political Neanderthal," he rumbled. "He would have been supremely happy in the court of Louis XIV. And the book to which you refer is a monumental exercise in fatuity." I sensed the subject was closed, so I grunted myself and turned to the sports pages.

I probably wouldn't have thought any more about that scrap of dialogue except now, three weeks later, a small, balding, fiftyish specimen with brown-rimmed glasses and a sportcoat that could have won a blue ribbon in a quilting contest perched on the red leather chair in the office and stubbornly repeated the statement that had persuaded me to see him in the first place.

"Hale Markham was murdered," he said. "I'm unswerving in this conviction."

Let me back up a bit. The man before me had a

name: Walter Willis Cortland. He had called the day before, Monday, introducing himself as a political science professor at Prescott University and a colleague of the late Hale Markham's. He then dropped the bombshell that Markham's death had not been a mishap.

I had asked Cortland over the phone if he'd passed his contention along to the local cops. "It's no contention, Mr. Goodwin, it's a fact," he'd snapped, adding that he had indeed visited the town police in Prescott, but they hadn't seemed much interested in what he had to say. I could see why: Based on what little he told me over the phone, Cortland didn't have a scrap of evidence to prove Markham's tumble was murder, nor did he seem inclined, in his zeal for truth, to nominate a culprit. So why, you ask, had I agreed to see him? Good question. I must admit it was at least partly vanity.

When he phoned at ten-twenty that morning and I answered "Nero Wolfe's office, Archie Goodwin speaking," Cortland had cleared his throat twice, paused, and said, "Ah, yes, Mr. Archie Goodwin. You're really the one with whom I wish to converse. I've read about your employer, Nero Wolfe, and how he devotes four hours every day, nine to eleven before lunch and four to six in the afternoon, to the sumptuous blooms on the roof of your brownstone. That's why I chose this time to call. I also know how difficult it is to galvanize Mr. Wolfe to undertake a case, but that you have a reputation for being a bit more, er . . . open-minded."

"If you're saying I'm easy, forget it," I said. "Somebody has to screen Mr. Wolfe's calls, or who knows what he'd be having to turn down himself—requests to find missing wives, missing parakeets, and even missing gerbils. And believe me when I tell you that Mr. Wolfe hates gerbils."

Cortland let loose with a tinny chuckle that probably was supposed to show he appreciated my wry brand of humor, then cleared his throat, which probably was supposed to show that now he was all business. "Oh, no, no, I didn't mean that you were . . . uh, to use your term, easy," he stumbled, trying valiantly to recover.

"No, I, uh . . ." He seemed to lose his way and cleared his throat several times before his mental processes kicked in again. "It's just that from what I've heard and read, anybody who has any, uh, hope of enticing Nero Wolfe to undertake a case has to approach you first. And that I am most willing to do. Most willing, Mr., er . . . Goodwin." I braced for another throat-clearing interlude, and sure enough, it arrived on schedule. If this was his average conversational speed, the phone company must love the guy.

"I will lay my jeremiad before you and you alone, and trust you to relay it accurately to Mr. Wolfe. You have a reputation, if I am not mistaken, for reporting verbatim conversations of considerable duration."

Okay, so he was working on me. I knew it—after all, he had the subtlety of a jackhammer, but maybe that was part of his charm, if you could use that term on such a guy. And I was curious as to just what "information" he had about the late Hale Markham's death. Also, the word "jeremiad" always gets my attention.

"All right," I told him, "I'll see you tomorrow. What about ten in the morning?" He said that was fine, and I gave him the address of Wolfe's brownstone on West Thirty-fifth Street near the Hudson.

The next day he rang our doorbell at precisely ten by my watch, which was one point in his favor. I've already described his appearance, which didn't surprise me at all when I saw him through the one-way glass in our front door. His looks matched his phone voice, which at least gave him another point for consistency. I let him in, shook a small but moderately firm paw, and ushered him to the red leather chair at the end of Wolfe's desk. So now you're up to speed, and we can go on.

"Okay, Mr. Cortland," I said, seated at my desk and turning to face him, "you've told me twice, on the phone and just now, that your colleague Hale Markham did not accidentally stumble down that ravine. Tell me more." I flipped open my notebook and poised a pen.

Cortland gave a tug at the knot of his blue wool tie and nudged his glasses up on his nose by pushing on one lens with his thumb, which probably explained why the glass was so smeared. "Yes. Well, perhaps I should discourse in commencement about Hale, although I'm sure you know something of him."

When I'd translated that, I nodded. "A little. I know, for instance, that he was a political conservative, to put it mildly, that he once had a newspaper column that ran all over the country, that he had written some books, and that he was more than a tad controversial."

"Succinct though superficial," Cortland said, sounding like a teacher grading his pupil. He studied the ceiling as if seeking divine guidance in choosing his next words—or else trying to reboard his train of thought. "Mr. Goodwin, Hale Markham was one of the few, uh, truly profound political thinkers in contemporary America. And like so many of the brilliant and visioned, he was constantly besieged and challenged, not just from the left, but from specious conservatives as well." He paused for breath, giving me the opportunity to cut in, but because it looked like he was on a roll I let him keep going, lest he lose his way.

"Hale was uncompromising in his philosophy, Mr. Goodwin, which is one of the myriad reasons I admired him and was a follower—a disciple, if you will. And do not discount this as mere idle palaver—I think I'm singularly qualified to speak—after all, I had known him nearly half again a score of years. Hale took a position and didn't back away. He was fiercely combative and outspoken in his convictions."

"Which were?" I asked after figuring out that half again a score is thirty.

Cortland spread his hands, palms up. "How to begin?" he said, rolling his eyes. "Among other things, that the federal government, with its welfare programs and its intrusions into other areas of the society where it has no business, has steadily—if sometimes unwittingly—been attenuating the moral fiber of the nation, and that government's size and scope must be curtailed. He had a detailed plan to reduce the government in stages over a twenty-year period. Its fundamental caveat was—"

"I get the general idea. He must have felt pretty good about Reagan."

"Oh, up to a point." Cortland fiddled some more with his tie and pushed up his glasses again with a thumb, blinking twice. "But he believed, and I concur, that the president has never truly been committed to substantially reducing the federal government's scope. The man is far more form than substance."

That was enough political philosophy to hold me. "Let's get to Markham's death," I suggested. "You say you're positive his fall down that ravine was no accident. Why?"

Cortland folded his arms and looked at the ceiling again. "Mr. Goodwin, for one thing, Hale walked a great deal." He took a deep breath as if trying to think what to say next, and he was quiet for so long that I had to stare hard at him to get his engine started again. "In recent years, walking had been his major form of exercise. Claimed it expurgated his mind. Almost every night, he followed the identical course, which he informed me was almost exactly four miles. He started from his house, just off campus, and the route took him past the Student Union and the Central Quadrangle, then around the library and through an area called the Old Oaks and then—have you ever been up to Prescott, Mr. Goodwin?"

"Once, years ago, for a football game, against Rutgers. Your boys kicked a field goal to win, right at the end. It was quite an upset."

Cortland allowed himself a sliver-thin smile, which was apparently the only kind he had, then nodded absently. "Yes . . . now that you mention it, I think I remember. Probably the only time we ever beat them. We had a . . . Rhodes Scholar in the backfield. Extraordinary chap. Name escapes me. Lives in Sri Lanka now, can't recall why." He shook his head and blinked. "Where was I? Oh, yes. Anyway, you should remember how hilly the terrain of our campus is, which isn't surprising, given that we're so close to the Hudson. Innumerable times, Prescott has been cited as the most picturesque university in the nation. There are several ravines cutting through it, and the biggest one is named Caldwell's Gash—I believe after one of the first settlers to the area. It's maybe one hundred fifty feet deep, with fairly steep sides, and the Old Oaks, a grove of trees that looks to me like it's getting perilously decrepit, is along one side of the Gash. Hale's walk always took him through the Oaks and close to the edge of the Gash."

"Is there a fence?"

"A fence?" Another long pause as Cortland reexamined the ceiling. "Yes, yes, there had been—there was . . . years ago. But at some point, it must have fallen apart, and never got replaced. The paved, uh, bicycle path through the Oaks is quite a distance from the edge—maybe thirty feet—and there are warning signs posted. On his postprandial strolls, though, Hale sometimes left the path—I know, I've walked with him many a time—and took a course somewhat closer to the edge."

"So who's to say your friend didn't get a little too close just this once and go over the cliff?"

"Not Hale Markham." Cortland shook his small head vigorously, sending his glasses halfway down his nose. "This was a dedicated walker. He even wore hiking boots, for instance. And he was very surefooted—his age, which happened to be seventy-three, shouldn't deceive you. During his younger days, he'd done quite a bit of serious mountain climbing, both out west and, er, in the Alps. No sir, Hale would not under any circumstances have slipped over the edge of the Gash."

"Was the ground wet or muddy at the time?"

"It had not rained for days."

"What about suicide?"

He bristled. "Inconceivable! Hale reveled in life too much. His health was good, remarkably good for his age. No note of any kind was discovered. I should know—I checked through his papers at home. I'm the executor of his estate."

"What about an autopsy?"

"No autopsy. The doctor who examined the body said Hale died of a broken neck, a tragic consequence of the fall. He estimated the time of death to have been between ten and midnight. And the medical examiner set it down as accidental death. But there really wasn't any kind of an investigation to speak of. Most distressing."

"All right," I said, "let's assume for purposes of discussion that there is a murderer. Care to nominate any candidates?"

Cortland squirmed in the red leather chair, and twice he started to say something, but checked himself. He looked like he was having gas pains.

I gave him what I think of as my most earnest smile. "Look, even though you're not a client—not yet, anyway—I'm treating this conversation as confidential. Now, if you have *evidence* of a murder—that's different. Then, as a law-abiding, God-fearing, licensed private investigator, I'd have to report it to the police. But my guess is you don't have evidence. Am I right?"

He nodded, but still looked like something he ate didn't sit well with him. Then he did more squirming. The guy was getting on my nerves.

"Mr. Cortland, I appreciate your not wanting to come right out and call someone a murderer without evidence, but if I can get Mr. Wolfe to see you—and I won't guarantee it—he's going to press pretty hard. You can hold out on me, but he'll demand at the very least some suppositions. Do you have any?"

Cortland made a few more twitchy movements, crossed his legs, and got more fingerprints on his lenses. "There were a number of people at Prescott who . . . weren't exactly fond of Hale," he said, avoiding my eyes. "I'd, uh, chalk a lot of it up to jealousy."

"Let's get specific. But first, was Markham married?"

"He had been, but his wife died, almost ten years ago."

"Any children?"

"None. He was devoted to Lois—that was his wife. She was one of a kind, Mr. Goodwin. I'm a bachelor, always have been, but if I'd ever been fortunate enough to meet a woman like Lois Markham, my life would have taken on a Byronic richness that . . . no matter, it's in the past. As far as children are concerned, Hale told me once that it was a major disappointment to both him and Lois that they never had a family."

"What about relatives?"

"He had one brother, who has been deceased for years. His only living relative is a niece, unmarried, in California. He left her about fifty thousand dollars, plus his house. I've been trying to get her to venture here to go through Hale's effects—we can't begin to contemplate selling the place until it is cleaned out, which will be an extensive chore. Hale lived there for more than thirty years."

"Has the niece said anything about when she might come east?"

"I've talked to her on the phone several times, and she keeps procrastinating," Cortland whined. "When I spoke to her last week, she promised that she'd arrive here before Thanksgiving. We'll see."

"Okay, you mentioned jealousy earlier. Who envied Markham?"

He lifted his shoulders and let them drop. "Oh, any number of people. For one, Keith Potter." He eyed me as if expecting a reaction.

"Well, of course," I said. "Why didn't I think of him myself? Okay—I give up. Who's Keith Potter?"

Cortland looked at me as if I'd just jumped out of a spaceship nude. "Keith Potter is none other than the beloved president of Prescott." He touched his forehead with a flourish that was probably supposed to be a dazzling gesture of sarcasm.

"Why was Potter jealous of Markham?"

I got another one of those long-suffering-teacher-working-with-a-dense-student looks. "Partly because Hale was better known than Potter. In fact, Hale was arguably the most celebrated person in the university's history. And we've had *three* Nobel prize laureates through the years."

I nodded to show I was impressed. "So the president of the school resented its superstar teacher. Is that so unusual? I don't know much about the academic world, but one place or another I've gathered the impression that most colleges have a teacher or two who are often better known than the people who run the place."

"Unusual? I suppose not. But Potter—excuse me, *Doctor* Potter—is an empire builder. His not-so-secret goal is to sanctify his name by increasing the endowment to Prescott, thereby allowing him to erect more new buildings on the campus. The edifice complex, you know?" Cortland chuckled, crossed his arms over his stomach, and simpered.

"I don't mean to sound like a broken record, but that's not so unusual either, is it? Or such a bad thing for the university?"

"Maybe not," Cortland conceded, twitching. "If it's accompanied by a genuine respect for scholarship and research, uh, things that all schools aspiring to greatness should stress. But Potter desires, in effect, to upraise a monument to himself. That goal easily eclipses any desire on his part to improve the facilities purely for academic reasons."

I was itching to ask if the ends didn't justify the means, but Wolfe would be coming down from the plant rooms soon, so I pushed on. "How did Potter's obsession with buildings affect his relationship with Markham?"

Cortland sniffed. "Ah, yes, I was about to get to that, wasn't I? Potter had fastened on to Leander Bach and was working to get a bequest out of him—a considerable one. I assume you know who Bach is?" I could tell by his tone that I'd shaken his faith in my grasp of current events.

"The eccentric multimillionaire?"

"That's one way of describing the man. I prefer to think of him as left-leaning to the point of irrationality. And that was the rub: The talk all over campus was that Bach wouldn't give a cent of his millions to the school as long as Hale was on the faculty. He had the gall to call Hale a Neanderthal."

I stifled a smile, then shot a glance at my watch. "Mr. Wolfe will be down soon," I said. "And I—"

"Yes, I've been monitoring the time, as well," Cortland cut in. "And we've still got six minutes. Mr. Goodwin, as you can appreciate, my stipend as a university professor hardly qualifies me as a plutocrat. However, I've had the good fortune to inherit a substantial amount from my family. Because of that, I can comfortably afford Mr. Wolfe's fees, which I'm well aware are thought by some to border on extortionate. And I can assure you that this check," he said, reaching into the breast pocket of his crazy-quilt sportcoat, "has the pecuniary resources to back it. If you have any question about my financial condition, feel free to call Cyrus Griffin, president of the First Citizens Bank of Prescott. I'll supply you with the number."

"Not necessary," I said, holding up a hand and studying the check, drawn on Mr. Griffin's bank and made out to Nero Wolfe in the amount of twenty-five thousand dollars.

"That's just a good-faith retainer," Cortland said. "To show Mr. Wolfe—and you—that I'm earnest. I will be happy to match that amount on the completion of Mr. Wolfe's investigation, regardless of its eventuation."

I tapped the check with a finger. Our bank balance could use this kind of nourishment—we hadn't pulled in a big fee in almost three months, and I was beginning to worry, even if the big panjandrum wasn't. But then, he almost never deigned to look at the checkbook. Such concerns were beneath him. Even if Wolfe refused to take Cortland on as a client, though, it would be instructive to see his reaction to somebody else who tosses around four-syllable, ten-dollar words like he does.

Maybe I could talk somebody into making a syndi-cated TV show out of their conversations and call it "The Battle of the Dictionary Dinosaurs." All right, so I was getting carried away, but what the hell, it *would* be fun to see these guys go at it. Besides, I'd pay admission to watch Wolfe's reaction to Cortland's mid-sentence ramblings.

"Okay, I'll hang onto this for now," I said to the little professor. "It may help me get Mr. Wolfe to see you, but I can't guarantee anything. I'll have to ask you to wait in the front room while we talk. If things go badly—and I always refuse to predict how he'll react—you may not get to see him, at least not today. But I'll try."

"I'm more than willing to remain here and plead my case with him directly." Cortland squared his narrow shoulders.

"Trust me. This is the best way to handle the situation. Now let's get you settled." I opened the sound-proofed door and escorted the professor into the front room, then went down the hall to the kitchen to let Fritz know we had a guest so that he would monitor the situation. It simply wouldn't do to have people wandering through the brownstone.

That done, I returned to the office, where I just had time to get settled at my desk when the rumble of the elevator told me Wolfe was on his way down from the roof.

TWO

When Wolfe walked into the office, I was at my desk entering orchid germination records in the personal computer he had finally agreed to buy after getting tired of my badgering. He detoured around the end of his desk, slipped a raceme of yellow *oncidium barbatum* into the vase on his blotter, and carefully settled his seventh of a ton into the reinforced chair that had been custom made for him years ago.

"Good morning, Archie. Did you sleep well?" It was his standard eleven o'clock question.

"No complaints. Fritz tells me it rained buckets last night, but I'll have to take his word. As the night watchman said when they woke him after the bank had been robbed, 'I didn't hear a thing.'"

Wolfe huffed his opinion of my humor and rang for beer. "Before you get too deeply immersed in whatever your day's activities will be," I said, swiveling in his direction, "I'd like to discuss Hale Markham." He sent a glower past the *oncidium barbatum* in my direction but said nothing.

"You know, the brilliant champion of the far right who tumbled down that ravine last—"

"Archie," he said, mouthing the word as if it were a communicable disease, "I can conceive of no reason why Hale Markham should be the subject of a discussion in this room."

"Well, try this on and see how it fits: The man was murdered."

His eyes bore in on me, unblinking. "Is this flummery?"

I tried to look hurt. "Am I the flummoxing type? No, sir, I have it on good authority—well, *reasonably* good authority—that the professor may have been helped to the bottom of that ravine."

Wolfe scowled. He was waiting for two things: beer, to be delivered by Fritz Brenner, and an explanation, to be delivered by me. He got the beer first—two chilled bottles and a glass on a tray. Fritz set them on the desk in front of Wolfe as usual, then did a snappy about-face and marched out. Wolfe took the opener from his center desk drawer, popped the cap on one bottle, and poured, watching the foam settle.

"On whose authority?" he demanded, returning his attention to me.

"There's a man sitting in the front room who says he was a colleague of Markham's at Prescott. Name: Walter Cortland. Occupation: political science professor. He came to see me this morning and gave me this." I got up and set the check in front of him.

Wolfe fingered it, drained half the glass, and resumed his scowl. "All right, report," he grumbled.

When Wolfe tells me to report, he almost always means verbatim, which isn't hard for me. As Cortland had mentioned when he was buttering me up, I've been known to repeat hours-long conversations to Wolfe without missing a comma. And I don't even own a tape recorder.

This one was a snap, of course, and after I finished, Wolfe leaned back. "It's hardly necessary to mention that the man in the front room is your problem," he said offhandedly. "You undertook to invite him here without consulting me. Further, nothing in your conversation with him in any way buttresses his claim that Mr. Markham was helped to his death."

I wasn't about to give up. "Through the years, you've complimented me at least twice—make that three times—on my ability to play hunches. Call this a hunch."

"No, sir, not good enough," Wolfe sniffed, reaching

for his current book, *In Hitler's Germany*, by Bernt Engelmann.

"Before you get comfortable, I'd like to point out that the bank balance is at its lowest point in the last ten months," I said, pulling the checkbook from my center desk drawer and shaking it at him. "I know you find it distasteful to worry about such mundane things as money, and I also know how repulsive you find work. But I remind you that you have to continue paying my princely wages, as well as those of Mr. Brenner, whom we agree is the finest chef in both hemispheres, and Theodore Horstmann, whom you claim has no parallel as an orchid tender. On that one, I'll have to take your word. Then there's the electricity, telephone, heat, and air-conditioning for this old brownstone, to say nothing of the bills from the butcher, the various other food purveyors, the beer distributor, the—"

"Archie, shut up!"

"Yes, sir."

"You may thank Mr. Cortland for taking the time and trouble to come here. You may also tell him that I have no intention of seeing him."

Now it was my turn to scowl, and I like to think I learned from a master. "All right, I resign," I said, in what I hoped was a level tone. "I'm a man of action—remember? At least that's why you hired me and how you've frequently referred to me. Well, the most action I'm getting in this house lately is the exercises I do in my room before breakfast, unless I count watching you drink beer, which I grant is a singular experience. Now, how do you want my resignation? I can type it out, or make a computer printout, or will a handwritten note be sufficient? Normally, I'd give two weeks, but I've got some vacation time saved up, and—"

"Archie!" It was almost a bellow.

"Actually, I've been thinking about going out on my own, and Mr. Cortland has all the makings of a good first client," I went on, ignoring him. "The publicity will be good for me, seeing as how I'll just be starting out. By the way, I hope on future cases I can use you as a character reference—I'd really appreciate it. And I'm sure Lon Cohen will see that my work gets good play in the *Gazette*. He owes me a few favors, Lord knows, and I'll need all the help I can get to establish a name for myself in this rough-and-tumble business. I don't think you truly realize what a jungle it is out there, all the clawing and scratching . . ."

As I talked, I saw Wolfe reach under his desk for the buzzer, which was unusual, since he still had one unopened bottle of beer in front of him. Within seconds, Fritz appeared at the door.

"As I'm sure you are aware, there is a gentleman in the front room," Wolfe said. "His name is Cortland. Ask him to come in."

THREE

The door from the front room into the office swung open, and Fritz ushered Cortland in. Wolfe glanced briefly at the closed book on his desk, then considered the professor, whom I again seated in the red leather chair.

"Sir," Wolfe said, dipping his head an eighth of an inch, "have you had anything to drink?"

"No, I—"

"I'm not surprised. Mr. Goodwin sometimes falls short as a host. I apologize for him. What will you have?"

Cortland shifted nervously, looking at me and then back at Wolfe and probably wondering how we coexist under the same roof. I've been wondering the same thing myself for years.

"I—what I started to say is that your . . . Mr. Brenner, isn't it? . . . offered me refreshments while I was in the other room, but I, uh, declined. Thank you anyway." He shifted again, clearing his throat and fiddling with both tie and glasses.

Wolfe observed the vellications with a frown and poured his second beer. "Mr. Goodwin has reported your conversation to me, and I have a number of questions. Before I begin, however, I want to stress that I have not yet accepted this." He picked up the check and tapped it. "Until I do, and there is no guarantee whatever of that occurrence, you are not a client."

"I understand," Cortland said, swallowing and bobbing his head.

"Very well. Am I correct in stating you are morally certain that Hale Markham's fall into that gorge at Prescott three weeks ago was not accidental?"

"Yes, I am. Furthermore—"

Wolfe held up a palm. "Please, if I may continue. Your turn will come. I know what you told Mr. Goodwin, but I will ask at least one of his questions again: Why do you believe your colleague was murdered?"

Cortland took a deep breath. "Mr. Wolfe, Hale Markham was not the incautious type—in anything he did. And with his hiking and climbing expertise and experience, he certainly would not have slipped into the Gash."

"You misunderstand me, sir. At least for purposes of this discussion, I am not questioning *whether* Mr. Markham was forced over the edge, but *why*."

"I'm sure I don't have to tell you I've ruminated on that at length," Cortland said, rubbing his hands together nervously. My own hands were getting damp just watching him. "As I related to Mr. Goodwin in our interlocution, Hale had his share of . . . calumniators."

Wolfe winced at this verbiage and I hid a smile behind my hand. "Tell me about them," he said dryly.

We were treated to another show of squirming, leg crossing, and throat clearing. Cortland then repeated, in more or less the same words, what he had told me about Keith Potter and Leander Bach. Wolfe watched him through narrowed eyes, pausing twice to drink beer. "It's patently obvious how you feel about Mr. Potter," he said when Cortland had finished. "How well do you know him?"

"Well enough." Cortland shrugged. "Or perhaps I should say, 'As well as I want to.'"

"That says nothing, sir. Try again."

Cortland sat up straight, twitched his shoulders, and sighed to indicate his irritation. "Keith Potter is an opportunist above all else. That was apparent from the day he stepped onto the Prescott campus. He was all smiles and glad-handing, and as far as I'm concerned, that's all he's ever been in the three years since he assumed the presidency."

"Then you observe him in action a great deal?"

Another sigh. "Enough. Mostly at receptions and, er, assemblies and faculty meetings. A congressional candidate would do well to take lessons from him. I realize that university presidents have to be diplomatic and personable—it comes with the territory. After all, one of their major duties is to importune wealthy alumni and irascible tycoons like Leander Bach. I don't quarrel with that. But as far as I can discern, that's about all Potter is good at—coaxing contributions out of nabobs."

"Is he capable of killing someone?" Wolfe almost purred.

"I've thought about that, of course," Cortland said, setting his jaw. "I don't like him one minim, as you have indeed observed, but I scarcely conceive Keith Potter would have the audacity to do such a thing, even if eliminating Hale would almost surely clear the way for a munificent bequest from Bach."

"And with Mr. Markham's death, is that bequest now forthcoming?"

"Nothing has been said officially, and I have heard no talk around campus. I suspect Potter will get Bach to come around now, but he's waiting what he considers a decent interval after Hale's demise to make the announcement. I say we can do very nicely without the largess of Leander Bach."

Wolfe rang for more beer, then readjusted his bulk. "How did others at Prescott feel about Mr. Markham?"

Cortland put his palms together and closed his eyes, clearly pondering a weighty question. The guy was really a piece of work. "Mr. Wolfe," he answered in a voice just above a whisper, "I don't know the extent of your knowledge of university faculties, but their members can be appallingly petty—individually and corporately. Prescott is no exception. And if you happen to be politically conservative, that pettiness is particularly glaring."

"That sounds like paranoia," Wolfe remarked.

"Paranoia? Hardly. Hale Markham is arguably the most famous faculty member the school has ever had. He has—had—been on our faculty for almost forty years, and had garnered international attention for most of that period. He'd been widely published, both academically and in the popular press. Yet he was never, not once, offered the chairmanship of the Political Science Department, even though that chair has changed hands four times in the last nineteen years." Cortland let loose of this damning fact and sank back into his chair triumphantly.

If this evidence of academic injustice shocked Wolfe, he kept it well hidden. "Are you suggesting a left-leaning conspiracy against Mr. Markham?"

"Don't mock me, Mr. Wolfe," Cortland shot back. The little guy had a spine after all. "The fact is, Prescott, like most schools, has a strong liberal-Socialist bias within its faculty, and to some degree in the administration as well. If you don't subscribe to their ideologies, there are a hundred ways you can be passed over, slighted, ignored, frozen out, cut down. Believe me, I know."

Wolfe's right index finger had begun tracing circles on the chair arm, an unmistakable sign he was losing whatever patience he had started this encounter with. "Sir, let us get down to cases. You came here because you contend that your colleague was the victim of a willful act of murder. So far, you have provided little in the way of suspects. Can you suggest someone within the university? Or anyone else, for that matter?"

"I am hardly an authority on murder, Mr. Wolfe. I don't pretend to divine the machinations of the criminal mind. That's why I came to you. I can only tell you about those people who disliked Hale."

"Do so."

"Besides Potter, there was Orville Schmidt, for one—he's chairman of the Political Science Department. He had been jealous of Hale for years."

"Because of Mr. Markham's prestige?"

"That's part of it, yes. I've heard him more than once in meetings and social gatherings refer sarcastically to

Hale as 'our local celebrity.' Never to Hale's face, mind you—he was always cordial to Hale in person, even deferential, but then, that's Orville for you: as two-faced as Janus himself."

"And Mr. Schmidt's political philosophy?"

Cortland screwed up his face. "Orville has always fancied himself as a profound liberal thinker. He's written a number of articles about how Socialism is"—he paused to shudder—"an inexorable tide that will ultimately engulf the Western World. And of course there was his book on FDR's social justice policies and programs," he said, not bothering to keep the contempt out of his voice. "Eight hundred pages and not an original shred of research or an original idea. Little wonder it got such insipid reviews. And to make matters worse for Orville, it came out at almost the same time as Hale's *Bleeding Hearts Can Kill.* Did you read it, Mr. Wolfe?"

"Yes," he said, tight-lipped.

Cortland seemed oblivious to the reaction. "A brilliant volume—beautifully written, masterfully reasoned. God, how it galled Orville that Hale outsold him by—what?—twenty to one? Fifty to one? Maybe more. But poor Orville doesn't give up. Next month, he's got another book coming out—this one on George Marshall and his two years as Truman's secretary of state, you know, the Truman Doctrine and all."

Wolfe drew in a bushel of air and expelled it slowly. "So you're suggesting Mr. Schmidt as a suspect, one driven by overwhelming professional jealousies?"

"Not necessarily," Cortland squawked defensively, jerking upright again with all the coordination of a marionette. "But he did resent Hale, maybe more than anyone else on campus. And the piece Hale did on his FDR book didn't help any."

"Tell me about it."

Cortland hunched his shoulders. "Even *I* thought Hale was astray on that one. He wrote a satirical little article about Orville's book for a small conservative journal. It was well-written, of course—everything Hale ever did was. And it was humorous, in a devastating way. Orville was absolutely livid. He thought the piece held both him and his book up to ridicule."

"Did it?" Wolfe asked.

"You'd have to say so. Granted, the book didn't have a lot to recommend it, but this article, which Hale later claimed was meant to be tongue-in-cheek, was pretty mordacious. Hale told me that Orville telephoned him at home in an absolutely uncontrollable rage, accusing him of taking a cheap shot at a colleague."

"And Mr. Markham's response?"

"Hale said he told Orville to loosen up, that the thing was intended as a joke, but that seemed to serve only to infuriate Orville further. The result was that the two were even more antagonistic to each other than they had been heretofore. Or rather, Orville was more antagonistic. I think Hale was indifferent and didn't care one way or the other what Orville thought. He seemed to relish tweaking people. That's part of the reason he made enemies."

"There were others?"

"Oh, yes. Again, at the risk of repetition, when someone on a university faculty is successful, particularly outside the academic world, as Hale indeed was with his books and newspaper columns and television appearances, the envy very quickly becomes palpable among his colleagues. And this is especially true when the successful person is a conservative. It drives the Jacobins crazy." Cortland's voice was somber, but the smug look on his face gave him away—the kind that probably made his liberal colleagues itch to punch him out.

Wolfe looked grumpy. I knew he was thinking about lunch—at that precise moment Fritz probably was sautéing the veal cutlets, which we were having along with endive salad. And although we occasionally invite clients to join us in the dining room, I could tell Wolfe was in no way about to add our present guest to that privileged group. "Mr. Cortland," he said, "so far, you've mentioned two purported enemies, at least philosophical ones, of your late colleague—three, if you count Leander Bach.

Based on what you've told us, hardly a bumper crop. Can you add to it?"

Cortland's cheeks turned pink. "I'm sorry. I guess I haven't been a great deal of assistance, have I? It has been excessively frustrating for me, too: I know beyond question that Hale's death was no accident, but I feel uncomfortable singling someone out and suggesting there is even a small chance he might harbor enough ill will against Hale to contemplate murder."

"You came here seeking help," Wolfe growled, turning a palm up and looking disgusted. "Mr. Goodwin felt your concern was justified and your conviction warranted. Through a device not worthy of mention, he inveigled me into seeing you. At this moment, you are in peril of losing my attention, however." Wolfe reached into his vest and pulled out the platinum pocket watch he almost never consults, setting it deliberately on the desk blotter. "You have two minutes to regain that attention."

Cortland went into an accelerated version of the squirming routine again before settling down. "Well . . . people who didn't like Hale. All right, another one was Ted Greenbaum—he's also in the Political Science Department.

"For that matter, Hale didn't like *him* either. Ted's in line to be the next chairman of the department—at least that's how it looks to most of us. Years ago, he was a student of Hale's—Ted positively idolized Hale. He was three years behind me at Prescott." He shook his head as if referring to someone who had gone on to that big classroom in the sky. "I never would have believed his metamorphosis if I hadn't seen it and experienced it."

"You are of course speaking about his philosophy," Wolfe translated.

Cortland nodded. "After graduation, Ted went off to Stanford for a doctorate, then taught at one of those excellent small colleges in Ohio—Kenyon or Oberlin, if I recall correctly—for a few years before coming back and joining our faculty. Those were great times, with Hale, Ted, and me all teaching and giving seminars and writing. In a cover story on 'The New Right,' *Time* magazine even called us 'Prescott's All-Star Team.' That mention really irked the hell out of left-wing faculty members, and the school administration, too."

"But somewhere along the way, Mr. Greenbaum became an apostate?"

"Lord, I haven't heard that word for ages," Cortland said, gazing admiringly at Wolfe. Realizing he had been distracted, he hurried on. "But, yes, that's exactly what Ted became. About eight years ago, maybe nine, he turned his back on us, and for that matter on everything to which he'd previously been dedicated. I've never seen anything like it. His shift seemed to come virtually overnight. I think it hit Hale almost as hard as Lois's death."

"What motivated the change?"

"Ambition," Cortland said with feeling. "I didn't see it in him earlier, but Ted was driven to be a success above all else. And he apparently felt that even though the three of us had received generous accolades, being a conservative at Prescott was not the way to get ahead in the academic world. I've always suspected Orville was the big influence behind his left turn, although I can't prove it, and I'll be damned if I'd ever ask either one of them about it." He crossed his thin arms defiantly.

"How did Mr. Greenbaum get along with Mr. Markham after his defection to the liberal camp?"

Cortland's expression was an answer in itself. "About the way you would expect. Hale thought of him as a turncoat, which is of course what he was. In departmental meetings, they sniped at each other incessantly, and Orville, who presided, pretty much let them have at it without interceding. I think he enjoyed seeing Hale get exercised."

Wolfe was looking even grumpier than before. "I don't suppose you can think of any reason Mr. Greenbaum would want to push your mentor over a precipice?"

"Not really," Cortland said, frowning. "He's an unprincipled ass, and he and Hale hadn't spoken a civil word to each other for years. But as for murder . . ."

"I thought as much," Wolfe muttered, gripping the chair arms and levering himself upright. "Sir, I must excuse myself because of a previous engagement."

"But what about Hale? What next?"

"What indeed?" Wolfe said, shooting me one of his I'll-deal-with-you-later looks. "I suggest at this point you and Mr. Goodwin decide on a course of action." Cortland, who now was on his feet too, began to sputter, but his protests bounced off the broad expanse of Wolfe's back as he passed through the doorway and into the hall.

"He's angry at me, isn't he?" Cortland whined. "But I was only being honest. As was obvious, I have a good deal of antipathy toward the men I mentioned, but I veridically have a difficult time picturing any of them—or anybody else I know, for that matter—as villainous enough to carry out a premeditated murder. That's why I came here in the first place. In the hopes that he, and you, of course, could cut through this conundrum."

"That's the business we're supposed to be in, all right, cutting through conundrums." I was beginning to wonder if the little professor ever tried to say anything simply. "Let's not be too hard on Mr. Wolfe, though. At this very moment, his brilliant mind is no doubt shrewdly processing the things you told him. I'll discuss the situation with him this afternoon and call you. My thinking right now is that I'd like to go up to Prescott, see the place where Professor Markham fell, and meet the people you mentioned, along with any others who knew him well."

Cortland looked troubled. I actually began to feel sorry for the sawed-off savant. "I don't think I'd want to broadcast the fact that I was hiring you . . ."

"Of course not," I said. "We can work out a plausible explanation for me to be there. Let's worry about that tomorrow. By the way, because Mr. Wolfe still hasn't made a formal commitment, you may want this back." I held out his check.

He shook his head vigorously. "No, no, please keep it. I still want to engage Mr. Wolfe, and I'll leave the draft with you as good faith."

"Fair enough," I answered, sliding the check into my

center desk drawer. I got up and gestured Cortland toward the front door. Wolfe wasn't the only one in the brownstone whose stomach was primed for Fritz's veal cutlets and endive salad.

FOUR

I was sore at Wolfe for walking out on our meeting with Cortland, but I knew he was getting back at me for trying to stick him with some work. To make matters worse, I couldn't even retaliate at lunch; he has a rule, never broken, that business is not to be discussed during meals. Consequently, I was a captive audience of one while he held forth on how the role of the vice president should be redefined to give him—or her—far more of the ceremonial duties of the executive branch, thereby freeing up the president to spend more time on the business of governing. I mainly listened and nodded while polishing off three helpings of the veal and two healthy wedges of blueberry pie.

When we were back in the office with coffee, though, I wasted no time getting on Wolfe's case. "Okay, so you're riled that I brought in a prospective client without checking with you first. And you also didn't much like the resignation business. But you've often told me how important it is that a guest be honored—'a jewel resting on the cushion of hospitality,' if I may quote you. Well, you certainly didn't treat Cortland like a jewel."

Wolfe took a sip of coffee and set the cup down deliberately, dabbing one corner of his mouth with a napkin. "Archie, I am accustomed to your febrile attempts at generating business without consulting me. That is hardly out of character. Further, I long ago became acclimated to your periodic resignations, one of which I may someday accept. Neither of those actions 'riled' me, to use your word. However, Mr. Cortland's performance this morning was patently irritating."

"You mean all those big words?" I grinned.

Wolfe waved away my question with a hand. "Bah. The man uses the language as if it were buckshot—indiscriminately and with little regard for precision. He obviously has gotten into the habit of using a big word where a small one will better serve him. My annoyance is far more basal."

"His refusal to suggest suspects?"

He shrugged. "Clearly, the dead man was not lacking detractors within the university community; this much we learned. The zealous disciple comes to us insisting that his oracle was murdered, yet is loath to single out an individual from among those detractors."

"So maybe he's concerned that he'll finger somebody who is innocent. That's natural enough," I said.

"Perhaps, although his obvious enmity toward those he identified might tend to preclude such concern."

"Are you suggesting that Cortland is a phony or a liar?"

Wolfe laced his fingers over his center mound. "Not necessarily. What do *you* suggest?"

I won't say Nero Wolfe never seeks my advice, but it probably happens less often than a presidential election, unless you count the times he asks my opinion about a young woman, particularly if she's a key figure in a case we're working on. He thinks I'm an expert on women, and I go on letting him believe that.

"I told you before that I'm playing a hunch here," I said. "I know you think I'm trying to drum up business, and I have to plead guilty to doing that more than once in the past. But I've got this feeling that little guy is on to something. Don't ask me to explain it—I can't. And I'm willing to put my money where my mouth is."

"Or is it my money?"

"No, sir, I mean it. I'd like to go up to Prescott. I'll even pay all the expenses myself, including the gas in your car. And for every hour I'm gone, I'll work an extra hour in the office for you on my own time. Fair enough?"

Wolfe raised his eyebrows. "What do you expect to accomplish there?"

"For one thing, I want to see the school, and the site of the so-called accident. For another, I'd like to meet those characters Cortland talked about today. Also, there must be others on the campus who knew Markham, probably knew him well. What about it? You've got nothing to lose."

Wolfe scowled. "How far is this place?" Despite his encyclopedic knowledge on a wide variety of subjects, he'd flunk a course in the geography of the New York metropolitan area, to say nothing of more distant precincts.

"About seventy-five miles north, an hour and a half at most," I said. "I know a lot of the country up that way, and it's a nice drive."

He shuddered at the idea of anybody willingly riding in an automobile for ninety minutes, let alone driving one. To Wolfe, people who use cars regularly have forfeited the right to be termed sane. I should mention here that he does own a car, a two-year-old Mercedes sedan that I had picked out. He can't drive it, and will only ride—in the back seat at that—when I'm behind the wheel. Even then, his trips out are rare, such as to the annual Metropolitan Orchid Show, which is all of twenty-five blocks from the brownstone. And even then, he keeps his eyes closed most of the way.

"When will you go?" he asked stiffly.

"I was thinking about tomorrow. I figure Cortland can show me around, and I'll use some kind of cover. Maybe I can be the father of a prospective student, there to take a look at the campus."

Wolfe frowned, maybe at the notion of me as somebody's father. "We're having spareribs for lunch tomorrow." It was a formidable objection.

"I'll have Fritz save me some," I said, but I didn't get a reply because he was behind his book, which meant he'd given up trying to talk me out of the expedition.

For the next hour or so, I entered orchid germination records into the PC, but at four o'clock, when Wolfe went up to the plant rooms for his afternoon playtime, I turned to my phone and dialed Lon Cohen's number at the *Gazette*. Lon doesn't carry a title at the paper, but he's got an office next to the publisher's on the twentieth floor, and when anything from a minor gang war to a bribery scandal in the mayor's office occurs, Lon seems to know more about it sooner than anyone else in the five boroughs. He answered in his usual world-weary tone.

"Nice to hear you sounding so chipper," I said. "Got a minute?"

"Of course not. What kind of trouble are you manufacturing today?"

"Hey, this is me you're talking to, remember? Archie, the newspaperman's best friend."

"Okay, friend, what's up?"

"What can you tell me about Prescott University?"

"What's to tell?" Lon said. "It's a private school, as I'm sure you know. Pretty campus. About halfway between West Point and Poughkeepsie, and they say the Prescott women prefer Military Academy cadets to Prescott men, while the men on campus would far rather go out with Vassar women than the ones at their own school. Enrollment's somewhere around six thousand, and the place has Ivy League pretensions—and Ivy League tuitions. Academically, so-so to good. For years, it was known for this archconservative, Markham, who just died in a fall a few weeks—wait a minute. Does this have anything to do with Markham, Archie?"

"Why would it?" I asked innocently.

"Just seems like a funny coincidence, that's all. A place like Prescott is lucky if it makes the papers once in five years—make that ten. Its most notorious faculty member tumbles into a ravine, and a few weeks later, one Archie Goodwin—the newspaperman's best friend, no less—calls and wants to know about the school. Now I ask, if you were me, wouldn't you be suspicious, too?"

"I might, if I were the suspicious type, like you. Fortunately, however, I'm not. Since you brought up Markham, though, what can you tell me about him? What kind of guy was he?"

"So you *are* interested in him." Lon's curiosity was kicking into high gear. "What gives?"

"Uh-uh," I said. "I've got nothing to share right now, but if and when I do, you'll be the first to know. What about Markham?"

I heard a sigh through my receiver. "Brilliant, although radical. He was somewhat trendy fifteen years or so back. That's when he was in demand as a speaker and columnist and a panelist on political TV shows. He was even approached to run for Congress from up around Prescott one time, but nothing ever came of it. You may remember that the *Gazette* carried his column for a while, but we dropped it, and so did a lot of other papers, and it finally died. The simple fact is that other conservative columnists like William Buckley and George Will are better writers and they aren't on the lunatic fringe, which is where I'd place Markham."

"What was he like personally?"

"I never met him, but from what I hear, cantankerous, contentious, inflexible. He didn't have much give in his political views, and he had the reputation as being hard to get along with on the faculty. He was quite an outdoor type, somewhat like that old Supreme Court justice from some years back, William Douglas. He'd done a lot of mountain climbing and hiking, as I recall. Also, I seem to remember hearing that he had quite an eye for the ladies."

"That doesn't make him a bad person."

"Not at all—probably helped keep him young. I think he'd been a widower for quite a number of years."

"Anything else I should know?"

"Isn't that enough?" Lon said. "I thought I'd done pretty well to dredge up what I did from memory. After all, he hadn't been in the news all that much in recent years. Archie, can't you give me at least a clue about what you're up to here?" Good old Lon. He never stops working.

"I wish I could, but you know how secretive the detective business is."

"Spare me, please. And remember who your friends

are when you finally decide you can talk about this for publication."

"That's a guarantee," I told him, and he knew I meant it. We've gotten a lot of helpful information from Lon through the years, but he's also built a thick file of *Gazette* exclusives, thanks to us. As Wolfe is fond of saying, on balance, we're more or less even.

After I signed off with Lon, I dialed Cortland's office number at Prescott, and he answered on the first ring. "It's Archie Goodwin," I said. "I'd like to come up there tomorrow. What time's most convenient?"

"Capital!" he squeaked. "I've got two classes in the morning, eight-thirty and ten-thirty, and my afternoon is completely free."

I told him I wanted to look around the campus on my own, and also that I hoped to meet Potter, Schmidt, and Greenbaum. There was a pause while he considered it. "I'm not sure about Keith, but I can probably introduce you to the other two, maybe at lunch in the faculty dining room," he said at last.

We talked some more, and it was decided that I would meet him in his office at eight o'clock the next morning. That would mean getting up about five, which is about two hours earlier than usual for me, but then, where does it say a detective's life is an easy one?

FIVE

The sun was just coming up on what promised to be a grade-A October day when I got the Mercedes from the garage on Thirty-fourth Street where we'd been keeping our cars for years. It was ten after six when I turned onto the Henry Hudson at Fifty-seventh and headed north, paralleling the river. The traffic was light as I crossed the George Washington Bridge and went up the Jersey side of the Hudson on the Palisades Parkway.

It felt good getting out of the city. Fritz had been popping his rivets with curiosity as I ate sausage, eggs, and griddle cakes and tried to read the *Times* at my small table in the kitchen. He frets when Wolfe isn't on a case because he thinks we're always three days from bankruptcy, and nothing I say ever seems to help. "Where are you going so early, Archie?" he asked anxiously, and when I told him, he asked if this meant we had a case. I hated to disappoint him by saying, in truth, that it was too early to tell, that this little venture north was strictly my own enterprise. He put on a glum face after that, but I calmed him somewhat by saying there was a possibility—only a possibility—that the trip might result in some business. At that I felt guilty, because I knew damn well no bookie east of Pittsburgh would give odds that I could get Wolfe to take Cortland's money.

I was on the Thruway now, having switched over west of Nyack, and was headed through the Ramapo Mountains, moving north with the semis, the RVs, and the station wagons with Maryland and Delaware plates and luggage on their roofs that probably were going up into the Adirondacks to ogle the fall colors.

On the phone with Cortland the day before, I had worked out a cover, discarding the father idea in favor of being an uncle. I was to be an acquaintance named Arnold Goodman, who was looking at Prescott as a possible school for my nephew, a high school senior in Indianapolis. "Normally, visits are planned through our Admissions Office," Cortland told me, "but because we're such 'old friends,' it would be perfectly commonplace for me to invite you up, show you around, take you to lunch. I can make all kinds of introductions with no trouble at all."

My watch read seven-thirty-five when I left the Thruway at Newburgh and turned east. When I got to 9W, I went north up the old road for about fifteen minutes, and at the bottom of a long grade found myself in Prescott, a small antique of a town that probably had a bed or two George Washington slept in. I vaguely remembered the place from that time some years back when Lily Rowan and I had come up for that football game with Rutgers, and it didn't seem to have changed a hair since. I drove along one side of the town square and, per Cortland's directions, found myself entering the campus of Prescott University, founded 1784, which matched some Hollywood producer's idea of how a college ought to look—redbrick buildings with spanking white shutters and spanking white columns and a sprinkling of ivy, set among lots of old trees that were changing their colors as proudly as any you'd find up in the Adirondacks or even Vermont.

I parked in the visitors' lot and, again following Cortland's directions, located the Union Building. Skirting one side of it on an asphalt path, I got to Richardson Hall, where his office was and where I was to meet him. It was three minutes to eight when I walked into an entrance hall that could have used a good airing, opened the frosted glass door on the first floor marked POLITICAL SCIENCE DEPT., and was greeted from behind a desk by a smiling, nicely arranged face framed by auburn hair. "Hi, can I help you?" the voice asked. It was nice, too.

"I'm here to see Professor Cortland," I said, using the smile that Lily once referred to as "puckishly engaging."

"Oh, you must be Mr. Goodman," she said, standing and letting me see that the rest of her also was nice. "Doctor Cortland is expecting you, but he's got a student in with him. He shouldn't be long."

I thanked her and took a hard-backed chair in the small reception area while she went back to typing, which gave me a chance to study her in profile. A particularly good nose, I thought, trying to remember which movie actress had one like it. I was concentrating on the problem when a shaggy-haired young man in blue jeans and a T-shirt with what apparently had once been a rock group's name on it passed me on his way out, followed by Cortland.

"Arnold!" he yelped as if greeting someone he hadn't seen since childhood. "Sorry to keep you waiting, but you know how crucial student conferences are."

"Walter," I said, rising and going along with the charade by pumping his hand vigorously. "I really appreciate your taking the time to see me." He ushered me past Ms. Auburn-Hair-with-the-Nice-Nose, and I turned to give her one last puckishly engaging smile, which got returned, with interest.

Once inside Cortland's office, which was roughly four times the size of a phone booth, I sat in the only guest chair while he slipped in behind his standard-issue metal desk. He was wearing a different crazy-quilt sportcoat from the one he had on when he visited us in New York, but the smudges on his glasses looked the same. "Here's a map of the campus that will facilitate your getting around," he said, handing it to me. "I've marked the important places."

"Thanks. I know you've got an eight-thirty class, so I won't hold you up. I want to see the place where Markham went over the edge, which of course I can do on my own, and I'd also like to sit in on a class taught either by Schmidt or Greenbaum, or both. Is that possible?"

"Why . . . yes, I suppose so," Cortland answered, looking surprised. "Let me check the schedule." He turned to a foot-high stack of papers on his right and burrowed into the middle of it, somehow coming out with what he wanted, a small booklet, which he thumbed. "Yes, I was pretty sure of this; Ted has the Introduction to American Government class at nine-thirty. That's an A-level course, principally freshmen. It's in the auditorium over in Bailey, with maybe three hundred students. You can slide in and hardly be noticed. As for Orville, let's see . . . he doesn't have any classes today—that's the department chairman for you. But I'll try to see that you make his acquaintance at lunch. He almost always eats in the faculty dining room."

I thanked Cortland and got up to go. As we were walking out of his cubbyhole, I nearly collided with a blonde in a jumpsuit who was lugging a stack of books. "Oh, I'm awfully sorry!" she exclaimed, looking up at me with round blue eyes that didn't remind me of any particular actress, but looked like they belonged right where they were. If the first two women I'd seen were typical of Prescott, I might just take residence here and wire Wolfe to find a new gofer.

The blond, whose head barely reached my chin, apologized again and turned to Cortland. "Excuse me, Professor, I didn't mean to interrupt. I wanted to see you before your class, about my paper—the one on Socialism and monetary policies in Germany between the wars."

"Certainly, Gretchen," he said to her. "I'd like to have you meet an old friend of mine . . . Arnold Goodman, who's up here scouting the school for his nephew. Arnold, this is Gretchen Frazier, a graduate student—our *star* graduate student, I might add."

Gretchen blushed prettily, then turned to me, smiling and holding out a hand. "I'm happy to meet you, Mr. Goodman. And again, I'm sorry. I've got to learn to slow down and look where I'm going."

"Only if you promise not to lose your enthusiasm in

the process," I said. "Walter, I'll leave you now; I know how busy you are."

"Fine, enjoy your look around, and I'll meet you after my ten-thirty class. It's in Bailey, room two-sixteen. We usually let out about eleven-twenty." I said good-bye and left the professor and the star student, who already had started in on him with rapid-fire questions about her paper as I walked down the hall.

If anything, the morning had gotten even nicer, and the air was filled with those woodsy smells you never get in Manhattan unless you're daring enough to explore deepest Central Park. Using Cortland's map, I made my way along a path toward the library, passing boys in everything from coats and ties to attire better suited to guerrilla warfare, and girls in the full range from skirts and heels to cutoff jeans and thongs. For the first time in years, I wondered, if only for a second, what I missed by not going to college.

I found the library easily enough—it was done in the same academic architecture as most of its neighbors, except larger and with more columns across the front. I swung around the left side of the building, as Markham had done on his evening strolls, and sure enough, there was the Old Oaks area. Cortland was right, the big trees here looked as if they'd be prime candidates for firewood before long. There were five of them, grouped more or less in a circle about a hundred feet across, and their branches all came together up high, forming a sort of vaulted shelter. I walked along a paved path covered with fallen leaves, stepping aside for an occasional biker with a backpack, and spotted the place where Markham must have gone over the edge; it was about thirty feet off the path. There was a sign, all right. You'd have to be legally blind to miss the eight-inch letters, which said: BEWARE! UNSAFE—NO FENCE. However, undoubtedly because of what had happened, a fence was being built. Metal posts had been driven into the ground, and rolls of chain-link fence were piled nearby.

I walked to the edge and peered down into Caldwell's Gash. The sides were steep, but they had a lot of undergrowth clinging to them, and the ravine was heavily wooded at the bottom. It was easy to trace the route of Markham's fall. Several of the bushes at the edge of the Gash had a ragged look to them, as though something had hit them with great force; a number of branches were cleanly snapped off. A bridle path was barely visible through the trees and brush more than a hundred feet below at the bottom of the ravine. I backed up with a shudder, remembering that the *Times* story had said a horseback rider discovered the body a little after dawn the morning after the fall.

A plunge that far could easily kill someone, even with the trees slowing the body down, which made me wonder why a fence hadn't been put in years ago, after the old one had rotted away. Maybe they figured it would destroy the unspoiled look about the Old Oaks; more likely some pencil pusher thought it was too big an expense. I walked along the rim of the Gash for several hundred feet until I found the stairway shown on the campus map. It was wooden, with railings, and it zig-zagged down the steep side of the ravine. The only thing I could hear was the chirping of birds as I made the long trip down and walked along the bridle path, which was hemmed in on both sides by vegetation. The Gash itself was barely twenty feet wide at the bottom.

A couple on horseback wearing riding clothes trotted by and gave a "Hi!" and they didn't seem surprised to see someone on foot. I worked my way along the path to where I figured Markham had landed. Broken branches and bushes marked the spot and a circle about seven feet in diameter had been trampled and cleared of under-brush, probably by the police and the crew that took the body away. I wasn't expecting to find anything and I didn't. By next spring, the area would be totally over-grown again, with no sign that a man died there.

I doubled back along the bridle path, this time passing a lone rider who didn't bother to return my greeting, and puffed my way up the stairway, reminding myself to step up my morning exercises. At the top, I checked my watch. Nine-ten. Plenty of time to catch my breath before going to Ted Greenbaum's class.

The Bailey Hall auditorium had theater-type seats sloping gradually to a stage, which was bare except for a lectern and a blackboard. The room was about half-full when I went in at nine-twenty-eight and took a seat midway down on the far-right aisle. My closest neighbor was an attractive Oriental about three seats away. She looked at me without interest when I sat down, and did not return my smile. So much for engaging puckishness.

A bell somewhere in the building rang promptly at nine-thirty, and a very tall, stooped, slender specimen with a thin face and salt-and-pepper, Ollie North-style haircut strolled nonchalantly onto the stage, nodded, and got behind the lectern. Putting on a pair of half-glasses, Ted Greenbaum looked out into the audience as if preparing to address a funeral gathering.

"As I said Monday, we will devote today's hour to the disintegration of the Whig party," he began in a nasal voice, gesturing toward the blackboard—actually it was green—which had the words DEATH OF THE WHIGS printed neatly on it in chalk. "The American Whigs had a relatively short life span," he went on, pronouncing each word precisely, as if his listeners were hard-of-hearing. "The reasons for the party's demise are several. First . . ."

As he continued, I turned and looked around the hall. About half the students were scribbling madly in their notebooks. Most of the rest looked bored, and a few had slumped down in their seats with their eyes shut. One was clearly asleep.

Greenbaum's delivery was far from snappy, but then, I don't know how even David Letterman could make the Whigs sound like party animals. I digested a few phrases and some names like Harrison, Tyler, and Taylor, making a mental note to bring up the Whigs to Wolfe at dinner sometime, maybe tossing in a couple of reasons why they self-destructed for his edification. After about twenty minutes of listening to him drone on, I'd seen and heard enough of Greenbaum the orator. I could only hope Markham had been a more interesting lecturer.

Nobody seemed to pay any attention as I rose and walked up the aisle and out of the auditorium. On the steps of Bailey Hall, I paused and tried to figure out how to spend the rest of the morning when who should I see scurrying along the sidewalk but the hyperactive little blonde in the jumpsuit who had almost collided with me at Cortland's office. "Hello, Miss Frazier," I called out. "Remember me?"

She put on the brakes and turned, tilting her head to one side. "Oh! Mr. . . . Goodman, isn't it? Are you getting a good look at the school?"

"Fair," I said with a shrug. "I've just been sitting in on Professor Greenbaum's lecture."

Her nose wrinkled. "Oh, there are so many better people to hear. I suppose it isn't nice of me to say that, though, is it?"

"Why not? Honesty's frequently the best course. That way, you never need to worry about keeping your story straight. Say, do you mind if I ask what you're doing for the next, say, half hour?"

"Heading back to my room to work, what else?" She sighed, letting her shoulders sag. "The life of a doctoral candidate is far from exciting, I'm afraid, Mr. Goodman."

"If you can spare the time, I'd like to buy you a cup of coffee," I said. "I haven't met any other students, and I think I might get a better idea of this place from you than from going to a dozen lectures."

"Certainly if they're Ted Greenbaum's lectures," she said, laughing. "I don't know how much help I can be— I've only been here as a graduate student, but . . . okay, I guess it would do me good to talk to someone who comes from the real world for a change. The nearest place for coffee is the grill in the Union Building."

"Lead the way," I ordered, and less than two minutes later, we were seated in a booth in the oak-paneled grill, which was deserted except for a baby-faced redhead who was almost hidden by a pile of chunky textbooks and a forest of empty soft-drink bottles.

Gretchen Frazier had girl-next-door good looks and the kind of complexion that didn't need much help from cosmetics, which she fortunately knew. As the waitress took our order, I asked where home was.

"Illinois. A suburb of Chicago that you've probably never heard of," she said. "I went to the big state university in Champaign for my bachelor's degree, and I've been here for a little over two years."

"Going for a doctorate, you said?"

She smiled and nodded. "In political science."

"How did you happen to come so far from home?"

Her face, which had been mostly smiles up to this point, darkened. "Prescott has a good reputation in poli sci, and . . . and it had Hale Markham."

"He was really well thought of, wasn't he?"

"Mr. Goodman, he was a *genius*," she said, with a quaver in her voice. She looked down at the coffee that had just been put in front of her.

"I take it you had him for some of your courses?"

She nodded. "Yes. I was working very closely with him. I admired his views a lot—long before I ever met him. When I was an undergraduate at Illinois, I read everything he had written, at least everything I could get my hands on. I even went up to Chicago from school once to hear him speak. He thought the way I do, Mr. Goodman. He was the main reason I came here," she said with intensity as tears formed in the corners of her eyes. "But you want to know more about Prescott. You certainly didn't come here to hear me talk about Hale Markham." She swiped at her eyes and smiled at me bravely.

Little do you know, I thought, but I allowed the conversation to turn to the school in general—its students, the caliber of its faculty, its facilities—before I steered back toward Markham. I may have hit a vein of gold, if only by accident, and I didn't want to lose it. Soon I had her going strong on her idol again. It turned out that Markham had not only been her idol, he'd been her adviser, had worked closely with her in seminars and on independent studies, and had even helped her to plan her doctoral dissertation.

"I feel so lost now that he's gone," she continued woefully. "Not that Professor Cortland and a few others haven't been good to work with too, but I'd just like to quit and get away from here. But I know Hale would have wanted me to go on."

I sipped my coffee and looked at her. "I seem to remember reading that he accidentally fell down a ravine. Does that happen often here?"

She shook her blond head and gnawed her lower lip. "Never, that I know of. Every few years, or so I've heard, a student commits suicide by jumping into the Gash or one of the other ravines. But the school paper wrote that this was the first time anyone had fallen into one by accident and died. It seems ironic that it was Hale of all people."

"Why?"

"He was so . . . physically fit. He walked a lot, took care of himself. He was seventy-three, but he looked and acted much younger."

"Might it have been suicide, Miss Frazier?"

"Oh . . . I suppose that's possible, of course. I hadn't thought of that before you mentioned it, honestly. Nothing was ever said about a note, and I can't imagine why Hale would have wanted to . . . you know. But I guess that's a possible explanation."

"How else do you explain what happened?"

Gretchen shook her head, and this time a tear spilled down her cheek. "I can't, I can't, except to go along with what the police think happened. He must have stumbled and fallen." She looked down at her coffee cup and I reached across the table, squeezing her hand for solace. She had been close to Markham, no question about it. Was it simply a student's admiration for a strong teacher, or had there been something more between them? Remembering what Lon had said about Markham's proclivities—and using the uncanny perceptions about women that Wolfe claims I have—I put my money on the latter.

SIX

I stayed in the grill with Gretchen Frazier until we'd both finished our coffee and she had dried her eyes. She was embarrassed and started to apologize, but I told her never to regret a genuine show of feelings. Then we shook hands and she scooted off to study while I walked back to Bailey Hall to meet Cortland. I got to two-sixteen, which was my idea of a typical classroom, at eleven-fifteen, and quietly slipped through a door at the rear. Cortland was standing next to a desk up front, facing about twenty students. I took a seat in the back.

". . . and so," he was saying, "with Theodore Roosevelt newly in his grave, the Republicans, supremely confident of victory in the nineteen-twenty election, turned to a virtual nonentity from Ohio named Warren Harding."

"Thus proving they could win with *anybody*," piped up a guy in a turtleneck sweater, drawing a scattering of laughs.

"The humorous aspects notwithstanding, you make a salient point, Mr. Andrews," Cortland said with a thin smile. "The truth was, with World War I just ended and the country sated with sick old Wilson's sanctimoniousness, not to mention Europe's problems and the League of Nations, the party could indeed have picked almost anyone. Next time—" He was interrupted by the bell. "Next time, we'll look at the dynamics within the Republican party that led to the nomination of Harding.

Be ready to discuss it. And prepare to step into the Roaring Twenties."

After the students had clomped out, I walked up to Cortland, who was stuffing papers into his briefcase. "Now, I grant that my history and political science knowledge is pretty skimpy," I told him, "but along the way, I've learned a little about Harding—after all, I *do* come from his home state. What I want to know is, how are you, a faithful conservative, going to be able to make him look good to your students?"

Cortland let out one of his tinny chuckles. "I don't even try. There are limits to historical revisionism, Mr. Goodwin—or I guess I should say *Arnold*, shouldn't I?" He whinnied again. "I'm glad nobody's here with us. Believe me, I won't err during lunch, I promise."

"What's the lunch program?" I asked.

"The faculty dining room is in the Union Building. It's a short walk."

"I was just there," I told him. "Having coffee with Gretchen Frazier."

"Oh?" He shoved his glasses up his nose and eyed me with interest.

"I ran into her after sitting in for awhile on Greenbaum's lecture. I thought I'd get her impressions on the school, and guess what?—we ended up talking about Markham."

"I'm not surprised," he said dryly as we walked out of Bailey Hall and into the sunlight. Two students dashed by, arguing about Madonna.

"Why?"

Cortland pushed his glasses up again. "Gretchen is a good student—indeed, a superb one, as I said when I introduced you to her—although perhaps somewhat shallow intellectually. But she's also a coquette, and she flirted plenty with Hale—among others, I might add. But her frivolity backfired on her—to the point where I'm afraid she ended up quite infatuated with him."

"How did Markham feel about her?"

"He was *fifty years* older than she!" he rasped indignantly. "Hale always has been . . . drawn to good-looking women, but they tended to be considerably older than Gretchen Frazier."

"Why didn't you tell me about Miss Frazier before, when you came to New York?"

"I didn't think it was very important; I still don't," Cortland sniffed.

"You also said she flirted with Markham *among others*. Who were the others?"

Cortland colored slightly. "I feel as though I'm trafficking in gossip."

"Look, you can call it what you want to, but the fact is we're trying to find a murderer, remember? This was your idea, and if you expect to get anything accomplished, you're going to have to talk about things you may find distasteful."

"All right," he said, inhaling deeply and steeling himself. "There was talk at one time last school year that Gretchen might have been . . . er, *involved* . . . with Ted Greenbaum." He took another big breath, like a kid who had just unburdened himself of a terrible secret.

"An unlikely combination," I observed.

"Not much more unlikely than she and Hale," Cortland said.

"Except that I gather Gretchen and Markham were philosophically *simpatico*."

"Gretchen is a fine student—a scholar, make no mistake about that," he said, "but I've yet to be convinced of her commitment to conservative philosophy. Her dalliance with Ted last year—if indeed it was that—would seem to indicate an intellectual instability on her part."

"It would if you equate political views with libido," I said. "Is Greenbaum married?"

"Yes."

"Happily?"

"I don't know!" Cortland wailed in exasperation. "I'm really uncomfortable talking about people like this."

"Then I'll probably make you more uncomfortable," I said offhandedly. "You mentioned that Markham was drawn to women. If not to Gretchen Frazier, to anyone in particular?"

"Yes." Cortland nodded grimly. "Elena Moreau is her name. She's a tenured professor in the History Department."

"Am I right to assume *she's* single?"

"Widowed," he said. "Her husband was killed in Vietnam."

"I'd like to meet her."

"You very likely will. Elena usually has lunch in the faculty dining room, sometimes at our table. And here we are."

We took an elevator to the third floor of the Union, and entered a Colonial-style room with brass chandeliers and polished wood tables and chairs, and waitresses in starched white costumes scurrying around. You had to admit that on the whole the Prescott faculty had it pretty nice.

"There's a table for six over in that corner," Cortland said. "A group of us from Political Science and History usually sit together—the cast varies from day to day. But we occasionally have guests, so you shouldn't feel at all uncomfortable."

"I never do," I assured him as we got to the circular table, where one man, stocky, ruddy, white-haired, and with a high forehead, was already seated. "Orville, I'd like to have you meet an old friend, Arnold Goodman. He's in from Indiana, looking the place over. His nephew is thinking about coming here. Arnold, this is Orville Schmidt, chairman of our Political Science Department."

"Mr. Goodman." Schmidt smiled and rose halfway out of his chair and leaned across to pump my hand with his fat paw. "We'll try to be on our best behavior for you. After all, a prospective tuition may hang in the balance." He chuckled at his little joke and I grinned to show that I appreciated his insidiously witty humor. That appeared to cement our friendship. "Did you come east just to see Prescott?" he asked after I'd scanned the three-entrée menu and selected roast leg of lamb.

"No, I was in New York on business and tacked on an extra day," I told him.

"What business are you in, Mr. Goodman?" Schmidt asked as he lavishly buttered a roll.

"I'm an insurance investigator, with a company based in Indianapolis."

"Must be interesting work," he said. I was getting an answer ready, but fortunately the conversation was interrupted by Ted Greenbaum's arrival. Cortland went through the introduction routine again, and as we stood shaking hands, I realized Greenbaum was easily six-five, or would have been if he stood straight. I told him I'd been in his lecture that morning.

"I know," he said with a crooked smile. "I noticed you, of course. And I'm afraid I must have bored you, judging by the length of your stay."

"Not at all. It's just that I wanted to see as much of the campus as—"

Greenbaum laughed. "You don't have to apologize, Mr. Goodman. The Whigs are not one of my favorite topics, either." In this setting, he didn't seem quite so dry and humorless.

"Oh, I don't know, Ted, I think you'd make a pretty good Whig," Schmidt said with a wheezing chuckle. "Personally, I've always been struck by your resemblance to William Henry Harrison."

"Our one-month president," Cortland chimed in with relish. "He caught his death of pneumonia because he insisted on delivering a three-hour inaugural speech in the rain. Maybe you'd better shorten your lectures, Ted."

Greenbaum was about to defend himself when we were joined by an attractive, exotic-looking brunette with her hair parted down the center and pulled back to show off large gold hoop earrings. She could have been anywhere from thirty to fifty. "Mind if I crash this stag party?" she asked in a slightly husky voice.

"Of course not, Elena," Schmidt said, polishing off his third roll. "We never do mind. And would it make any difference if we did?"

"None at all," she replied, winking and sliding into a chair.

"Elena, we have a guest today, so try to behave yourself," Greenbaum said. "This is Arnold Goodman, a friend of Walter's; he's looking the place over for a nephew who feels, oddly enough, that he might like to tread these sacred halls. Mr. Goodman, meet Elena Moreau, who's in the History Department, but we let her sit with us occasionally anyway. We feel it'll do her good— a little of our erudition might actually rub off on her someday."

"The only thing from any of you that's likely to rub off on me is cobwebs," she fired back with a wicked smile. "Mr. Goodman, I'm glad to meet you, and I apologize for these Philistines. Lord knows, I've tried to work with them, but . . ." She shrugged expressively. "Your nephew—what is he thinking of majoring in?"

"I hadn't mentioned this to Walter before, but . . . well, history," I said, inspired.

"Voilà!" Elena looked around the table triumphantly. "Sounds like a young man who's done his homework. *He* knows where the strength of this university lies."

The three men groaned, but it was good-natured, and soon all four professors were involved in a lively skirmish about the latest presidential polls. Despite what Cortland had told me about both Schmidt and Greenbaum, I noticed that he seemed to get along with them well, although maybe he was on his best behavior with an outsider present. I was glad to be out of the spotlight as they talked—that way I was able to observe all of them, particularly Elena Moreau, who was definitely worth observing. I now put her at somewhere in her early forties, but that didn't bother me—quite the contrary. Her dark eyes danced when she talked, and her oval face was full of expression. If Markham had indeed been playing games with her, as Cortland suggested, I gave him good marks for his taste. May I be thus blessed at age seventy-three.

Their banter went on for several minutes, until I noticed Cortland look over his shoulder. "Ah, our noble leader is present," he said. He gestured toward a figure who was standing just inside the entrance to the dining room.

The newcomer was maybe six-one, slender, dark-haired, moderately handsome, and wearing a brown suit that probably set him back at least five bills. He looked around, then waved and headed for a table on the far side of the room.

"That, Mr. Goodman, is our president, the right honorable Keith Alan Potter, B.A., Dartmouth; M.A., Harvard; Ph.D., Oxford, and don't you forget it," Elena said. "We would have been happy to introduce you, but for some reason, he never condescends to join our little salon."

"Now, be fair, Elena," Schmidt admonished seriously. "You know he has a lot of commitments, even at lunch."

"Such as sharing a table with his provost and dean of students—the same people he eats with every day?"

Schmidt shrugged and reached for the last roll. "The business of running the university never ends."

"Business, my Aunt Matilda," Elena snorted. "Look at the three of them huddled together laughing over there. I've got five dollars that says they're either telling the latest sleazy ethnic joke or figuring out which teams to take Sunday in that pro football pool Charley runs—Charley's the men's dean, Mr. Goodman. He majored in odds making at Colgate."

"As you can see, Mr. Goodman, Elena is our caustic wit," Schmidt said. His face smiled but his voice distinctly lacked humor. Clearly Elena's criticisms of Potter were hitting a sore spot. Before I could respond, Greenbaum, who was on my right, turned and asked about my business. I got away with a few generalities on insurance investigation that seemed to satisfy him; meanwhile, the others started in on whether Prescott should make a concentrated effort to increase its enrollment. Schmidt voted yes, claiming that it was essential the school grow by at least one thousand students over the next few years, which apparently was the party line as espoused by Potter.

Both Elena and Cortland took the other side, contending that Prescott was if anything too large already. Greenbaum pretty much stayed out of the discussion, although I couldn't tell if it was from boredom or simply because he had no opinion.

"I think we've talked about this long enough," Elena said at last, turning her lively eyes on me with what I translated to be interest. "Mr. Goodman, have you seen enough of Prescott so far to form any opinions? What are you going to tell your nephew?"

"I'm still doing research," I answered. "And you can help me, if you will. If you have a few minutes after lunch, I'd like to ask you about the History Department."

"Careful what you say, Elena. Remember, he *is* an investigator," Greenbaum admonished, signaling for more coffee.

"Let him investigate," she challenged, smiling impishly. "I'll be on my guard, Ted. Yes, Mr. Goodman, I can spare a little time. Do you mind going back to my office? I've got to pick up some papers there."

I said that was fine with me as the group broke up. They each had separate checks, and Cortland picked mine up. We agreed that I'd meet him back in his office at two o'clock, and off I went with the exotic Mrs. Moreau. "My office is in Meriwether Hall," she said as I caught a whiff of a scent I couldn't identify, but liked. "Have you been there yet?"

"Nope. Richardson and Bailey, but not Meriwether."

"Well, don't get too excited," she said. "They're all pretty much the same—American Colonial on the outside and Academe Dreary on the inside."

Meriwether indeed looked like the other buildings, although it was set in a nicer grove of trees and had more ivy on its brick walls. Elena's office was on the first floor, and was barely bigger than Cortland's, but considerably neater. There was a color photo of the New York skyline at night on the wall facing her and another of the Golden Gate Bridge behind her. "See what I told you?" she said, gesturing me to a chair facing her desk and closing the door. "I think schools hire somebody to come in and make the interiors of all their office and classroom buildings as cheerless as possible."

"Could be worse," I said, grinning. "At least you've got a nice view. I appreciate your taking the time to see me."

She flashed that impish smile again. "Oh, I would have invited you over here if you hadn't invited yourself. I'm most curious as to what you're up to here at Prescott, Mr. Archie Goodwin."

SEVEN

I like to think very few things knock me off stride, but that did, and I probably showed it. "I beg your pardon?" was the best I could do in response, and Elena Moreau considered me with amusement from behind her desk.

"Mr. Goodwin, don't tell me you thought you could come up here, less than ninety minutes from New York, and not be recognized by someone. Don't you know that you're famous?"

"Tell me about it."

She shifted in her chair and her smile widened. "I thought you looked familiar when I walked into the dining room, but I couldn't place you right off. Then when I heard that silly name—Arnold Goodman, really!—it clicked. I've seen your picture in the New York papers two or three times, I suppose in connection with some case or another of Nero Wolfe's. At that, I should have recognized you anyway; we've met before."

"Ouch," I groaned. "In the words of somebody who's probably famous, that's the unkindliest cut of all."

"Shakespeare, by name, and the actual phrasing is 'most unkindest cut,'" she said, tossing her head so that her hoop earrings danced. She was having entirely too much fun. "We have a mutual friend, Mr. Goodwin."

"Call me Archie, please. Especially since you seem to know me so well. I do believe it's coming back, though. Would our mutual friend have the initials Lily Rowan?"

She chuckled. "Could be."

"Look, I admit you're holding the high cards, but give me a second to recover. Did I meet you at a Children's Aid benefit ball, six years ago—possibly seven—at the Churchill?"

"Bravo!" she said, clapping nicely shaped and well-manicured hands. "I can't swear to the year, but it was at the Churchill, and you were indeed with the charming Lily. And I can hardly blame you for not remembering me, either. Lily's beauty is enough to put everyone else around her in the shade."

"You do just fine yourself," I assured her. "And you may not believe this, but I thought I recognized *you* at lunch, too."

"Maybe I'll choose to believe it," she said with another toss of her head. "How's Lily? It must be more than a year since I talked to her."

"Just fine as of Saturday night. I was with her at, of all places, the Churchill, attending, of all things, a charity ball. How do you two know each other?"

"A number of years ago—never mind how many—I was on the faculty at City University, and she was in one of my classes. As I recall, she wasn't a full-time student, just taking a course or two that interested her."

"That's Lily, all right, always shopping."

"Anyway, we got to know each other, although I can't say we were close friends—we traveled in somewhat different social circles, to say the least. She did get me involved in some of her good works, though; one of them was Children's Aid, which was why I happened to be at that ball. By then I had switched over to NYU, but since I've moved up here—I've been at Prescott four years now—I don't see my old New York acquaintances all that often. But we're supposed to be talking about *you*, as in, why are you here?"

"To repeat what I said at lunch, I'm scouting the university."

"Right. That's why you were using an alias, and a pretty transparent one at that."

"Okay, so it wasn't terribly clever," I conceded.

"When I made it up, I didn't realize it was going to get critiqued so thoroughly."

"Mr. Goodwin—Archie—you don't really have a nephew in Indianapolis, do you?"

"No comment."

"If I may suggest a scenario," she said, leaning back, smiling, and lacing her fingers behind her head. "Try this: Walter Cortland, poor myrmidon that he is, thinks that Hale Markham was bumped off, to use your vernacular. He realizes there's little if any support for his contention at the school and less with the local police. So where does he go? To the world-famous sleuth Nero Wolfe in New York, the man hailed for his deductive miracles. And what does Nero Wolfe do, but—"

"Let me guess," I said, holding up a hand. "He sends his lackey—that's me—up to poke around."

"Bingo! Although lackey is a word that demeans what I understand to be your not inconsiderable talents. I prefer associate at the very least. And colleague is even better."

"Sounds good to me—colleague, that is," I said. "As for your scenario, it's amusing."

"What other explanation is there?" Her eyes twinkled mischievously.

"Okay, for purposes of discussion only, let's assume that you've got it more or less right. What do you think of the idea that Markham was murdered?"

"Absolute bunk," Elena Moreau said, turning instantly serious.

"Why?"

She leaned forward, resting her elbows on the desk, and fastened those big, dark eyes on me. "Archie, I'm sure you're aware that I knew Hale well—I like to think better than anybody at this university, or anyplace else, for that matter. And that includes poor, deluded Walter Cortland. A lot of people took issue with Hale, both for his political philosophies, not all of which I agreed with myself, and because he always said exactly what he felt. Diplomacy was not among his qualities, and his candor upset some people. But as far as somebody killing him . . ." She shook her head emphatically.

"Okay, since we're on the subject, how did he happen to tumble into Caldwell's Gash?"

Her face darkened. "I'm sure it will come as no surprise to you that I've thought about that a lot the last few weeks. Hale had had at least a couple of fainting spells a while back, around the beginning of summer. I tried to get him to see a doctor at the time, but he insisted it was nothing. I have to believe he may have had one of these spells when he was out on his walk . . . that night, and lost his balance. He often walked foolishly close to the edge of the Gash—I know, I've been with him occasionally on his strolls."

"Did you ever see one of his fainting spells?"

"Umm, twice. One afternoon we were walking across campus, and he stumbled. I thought he'd tripped, but he was actually blacking out, and I caught him, more or less, and kept him from falling. He was okay after a few seconds, but he was very embarrassed about what had happened. Hale's physical condition was a terrific source of pride to him, Archie. The other time, we were just leaving a restaurant in town after dinner, and he got dizzy on the sidewalk out in front."

"Had he been drinking?"

"One glass of wine. That's all he ever had. Part of his physical-fitness thing. Again, I asked him if he was all right, and he got very testy, said he hadn't slept well the night before, or something like that."

"Those were the only times he blacked out?"

She shrugged and straightened a pile of papers that didn't need tidying. "As far as I know, but I doubt very much if Hale would have told me about any others. He was chagrined enough as it was."

"Do you know if he'd had a checkup recently?"

"He had a full physical in April, and the doctor told him he'd never seen anyone his age in such good condition. Heart, lungs, blood pressure, cholesterol level, everything. And you know what else the doctor told him?" she demanded. "That he was almost a cinch to make it to ninety."

"And he didn't see the doctor, or any doctor, after these fainting spells?"

"Not that I'm aware of."

"Is suicide a possibility?"

"Not at all! Inconceivable. No reason for it. Hale was healthy, he was happy, he was reasonably fulfilled professionally—and I like to think his personal life was fulfilling, too."

"Do you have any other theories as to what might have happened?" I asked, letting my inquiries into Markham's personal life rest for a moment.

"No, just that he must have blacked out. As far as I'm concerned, it's the only possible explanation. I'd like to know why Walter is so certain it's murder."

"I never said he was. Remember, that's *your* scenario."

"Oh, come on, Archie," she said, using a voice that would have turned an iceberg into a puddle. "Can't we toss out this silly charade?"

"Speaking of your scenario," I said, ignoring her question, "why do you believe Cortland thinks Markham was murdered? Has he voiced any suspicions?"

"Not in so many words, but it's the way he's been behaving lately, the looks he gives us, as if he's trying to peer right through us. And then some of his comments during lunch are hard to miss. For instance, a few days ago when Hale's name came up in some context or another, as it does fairly often, of course, Walter made a remark about the *accident*. From the way he stressed the word, it was obvious he was suggesting the fall wasn't an accident. There've been other occasions like that, too."

"Who are the *us* that he gives strange looks to?"

"Oh, pretty much the ones who were at the table at lunch today."

"Speaking of which, did Markham used to be part of that luncheon gathering?"

"Hale? No, never. He preferred to have a sandwich in his office and get a little writing done during the noon break. Besides, he didn't much like some of the people who showed up there."

"Such as Schmidt and Greenbaum?"

"Right."

"How did he feel about you eating with those guys?"

"Oh, he probably didn't much like it; but Hale knew me well enough to realize that I do whatever I please. And although I'm not wild about any of those three—including Cortland—I don't mind eating with them." Her dark eyes defied me to make more of it.

"Probably because you enjoy needling them. I notice that you and Cortland seemed to agree on at least one thing: President Potter."

"Oh, you mean 'His Eminence'?"

"I gather you don't have a great deal of admiration for your president?"

Elena folded her arms. "He's sort of plastic, as far as I'm concerned. I suppose he's all right at raising money and giving speeches and putting on a good public face for the school, but we're not talking deep thinker here. I suppose maybe it's that he's a little too slick for my taste."

"What do others think about him?"

"On campus, you mean? Most of the students don't give a damn one way or the other about who the president is—they almost never see him. As for the faculty, the vote's mixed. A lot feel the way I do, and then there are some who seem to think he's dynamic, probably because he's so much younger than his predecessor. And the alumni are happy because of the way he's increased the endowment and is planning new buildings. Alumni are always impressed by two things—football and construction. Both give them a chance to beat their chests about the old alma mater. And with the kind of football teams we invariably have, new buildings are pretty important."

"Buildings as in Leander Bach?"

"Oh, you know about him, do you? Walter—or somebody"—her voice was sarcastic—"has done a pretty good job of briefing you. Then you probably also know that Bach had no use for Hale."

I nodded. "To the point where he wasn't going to crack open his checkbook while Markham was still part of the school, or so I heard."

"You heard more or less right," Elena replied crisply. "Bach is a blustering eccentric. Another one of those self-made millionaire pains-in-the-ass who dangle their money with all kinds of strings attached to it."

"Did he really try to get Markham off the faculty?"

"Oh, I don't have any doubt of it. Potter talked to Hale about three or four months back and suggested he might want to think about retirement. Bach's name never came up in the conversation, but Hale told me he was sure that was the reason behind it. He told Potter—in effect—to stuff it, that he was happy right where he was. The subject wasn't brought up again."

"And now the school will get Bach's bucks?"

"That's what I hear," she said, making a face.

"Which means of course that Markham's death was a boon to Potter."

"Now, wait just a minute, Archie," Elena said, angling forward in her chair. "You've been around violence for so long you think it's everywhere, which is understandable. And what with Walter Cortland whispering murder in your ear, I'm not surprised that you add two and two and get seven. Potter may be a jerk—hell, he *is* a jerk—but he's hardly a murderer. Remember, you're not in New York now."

"This may come as a shock to you, but the act of murder isn't confined to the five boroughs and a few blue-collar suburbs."

"Oh, I know. It's just that—let's stop right where we are," she interrupted herself. "I brought you over here to ask you questions, and for the last thirty minutes, I've been doing almost nothing but answering yours."

"You're right, and I appreciate it," I said, grinning and standing up. "I promise that at another time I'll do the answering, but I really have to go now, and besides, I've taken a lot of your valuable time. Can I ask a favor?"

"You may ask, but I won't guarantee anything."

"Please, for now, don't tell anybody who I am."

"You're absolutely convinced it's murder, aren't you?" Elena said, rising and folding her arms as if she were suddenly cold.

"Call it a strong hunch."

"All right, Mr. Archie Goodwin," she said, no longer smiling. "I'm not happy with all this secrecy of yours, especially after I've been candid with you. But I know enough about your reputation to know that you must have reasons, and besides, anybody Lily likes has got to be all right. I'll keep your secret. At least for now."

"And in return," I said, "I'll buy you dinner the next time you're in New York. That's a promise. And I'll also give your best to Lily."

"I accept the invitation. And tell Lily I pledge to call her soon." We parted with a businesslike handshake, which made two of those I'd had with attractive women in one day. Whatever became of the friendly embrace? I walked back to Cortland's office in Richardson Hall, deciding on the way that I would not tell him Elena knew who I was. No sense complicating the situation unnecessarily.

The auburn-haired greeter with the nice nose was still manning her desk in the Political Science Department reception area. She was on the phone, but when she saw me, she smiled in recognition, mouthed "He's expecting you," and motioned me to go on back. I made a mental note to shake hands with her on the way out.

Cortland was at his desk grading a stack of papers. He glanced up as I walked in, and his face looked a question mark at me.

"Well," I said, easing into the guest chair, "I can't honestly tell you I've made any great discoveries today, but I can say that I haven't ruled out murder."

He dropped his red pencil on the desk blotter. "And how did your meeting with Elena Moreau go?"

"All right," I said casually. "You said earlier that she and Markham had been . . . friendly?"

"Oh, yes," he said firmly, nodding. "I never discussed his private life with Hale, mind you, but I knew, like everyone else, that they were very close friends."

"Meaning lovers?"

Cortland cleared his throat. "I really haven't the faintest idea. You'd have to ask her that."

I pushed on, undaunted. "Do you have any idea how Elena Moreau felt about Gretchen Frazier?"

"None whatever," Cortland said in an offended tone.

"Okay. You mentioned when we first met that you're executor of Markham's estate. I assume you have a copy of his will?"

"Why, yes, I do. At home," he said absently. "Why?"

"I'd like to see it. If you could make a copy and mail it to Mr. Wolfe in New York, it might very well be of some help."

Cortland looked doubtful, but after I assured him the document would not be seen by anyone other than Wolfe and me, he promised to mail a copy that evening. I thanked him, getting up to go.

"Oh, one more thing," I asked, trying to make the question sound spontaneous. "Do you know what route was used to take Markham's body up out of the Gash?"

"I must say, that's a bizarre query." Cortland squinted at me through his smudged lenses. "But I, uh, suppose you detectives have a rationale for everything you ask. Let's see . . . I actually can supply an answer. It was mentioned in the story in what passes for a local newspaper here. They brought"—he shuddered—"Hale . . . up that wooden stairway not far from the Old Oaks."

"I thought as much. Thanks." I got up to go.

"When will I hear from you?" he asked, and I said it would depend on Wolfe. "My boss is a hard man to predict," I said. "But I'm sure we'll be talking about this whole business in the next few days. And if anything happens up here that you think I should know about, please call."

Cortland assured me he would, and I said good-bye, walking out past Ms. Auburn-Hair, who was off the phone. "I really hope you had a nice day here, Mr. Goodman," she said, flashing a smile that ranked right up there with Elena's.

"Thank you for asking," I said. "It was so nice that I just know I'm going to come back. And when I do, I hope we can have lunch or dinner together. I'll trust you to pick the place."

My answer was another smile, the kind that I chose to take for a yes with capital letters.

EIGHT

It was almost four when I left Prescott. The traffic going south was a lot heavier than when I was driving up, so it was after six when I finally eased the Mercedes into the garage on Thirty-fourth Street. When I got back to the brownstone, Wolfe was, naturally enough, parked behind his desk with beer and his book. He didn't bother to look up when I walked in.

"Well, aren't you even going to ask how my trip was?" I said after I'd gotten seated. "After all, I've been behind the wheel for close to a hundred-fifty miles, round trip, which in your eyes ought to qualify me for hazard pay."

"I seem to recall that the expedition was your idea," he said blandly, "and that you were more than willing to undertake it on your own time."

"True enough. I suppose if I told you that within an hour of arriving on the Prescott campus, I figured out who the murderer was, confronted said person, extracted a confession on the spot, hauled the guilty party off to the local police, and then collected a check for one hundred thousand dollars from Walter Cortland, I'd get your attention?"

Wolfe set his book down and glared. "Confound it, I don't want to hear about your peregrination at this moment. After dinner is soon enough." With that, the book went back in front of his face, so I sauntered out to the kitchen to monitor Fritz's progress on dinner, lamb chops with walnuts. So I would have lamb twice in seven hours, but that was okay with me.

"Archie, I was afraid you would miss two meals in one day." Fritz looked worried as he turned from the stove, where he was checking on the chops, which he cooks in wine with chopped onion and parsley. "How was your trip?"

"Tolerable, but if what you're really asking is whether we have a case and a client, that's going to depend totally on the large presence who's soaking up beer down the hall yet as we speak." The fretful expression on Fritz's face deepened as he pivoted back to his work, while I went to my room to clean up and get out of the suit I had been wearing for twelve-plus hours. I knew Fritz was seeing us as candidates for New York's homeless population.

Wolfe invariably sets the topic for dinner-table conversation, which is never business but can range from foreign policy and economics to the social structure in ancient Rome and the fluctuating price of coffee beans from South America. This time, though, I was able to set the agenda by bringing up Greenbaum's lecture on the Whigs, and damned if it didn't get Wolfe going. He started by saying the word was derived from *Whiggamore*, a seventeenth-century term used to describe Scotsmen who opposed King Charles I of Britain, and he went on, with me barely wedging a few sentences in, to talk about why the party dissolved in the United States in the years before the Civil War. I felt like I was listening to a repeat of Greenbaum, with one difference: Wolfe is one hell of a lot more interesting.

After dinner and dessert, which was peach pie à la mode, we sat with coffee in the office. "All right," Wolfe said, delivering one of those sighs meant to show how long-suffering he is. "Before you start badgering me, report."

I swung to face him, stifling a smile. "Yes, sir, from the beginning." I proceeded to run through the entire day, and as I described the cast of Prescott characters, his face reflected varying degrees of distaste. But then, his overall opinion of contemporary American education, including that at the university level, is probably somewhere in the D-plus range. When I finished it off by telling him that Elena Moreau had recognized me, he snorted. "Your repute appears to follow you."

"*My* repute? Your mug has been in the papers a lot more than mine has. If you'd been up at Prescott, someone would have recognized you even before you got out of the car. Hell, you're the best-known living American who's never been on the cover of *People* magazine."

He shut his eyes, probably hoping I would disappear, then opened them after five seconds. I was still there. "Is Mrs. Moreau likely to reveal your identity?"

"Nine-to-two against," I answered. "If she's not the murderer, she has no reason to blow my cover, and if she is, there's even less reason for her to finger me and make me suspicious of her."

"Assuming there was a murder, are you giving odds on her guilt?"

"Too early. Right now, my gut says probably not, but don't ask for concrete reasons; I don't have any."

Wolfe looked disgusted. I'll admit my instinct was pushing its luck with him these days. "What does your gut tell you about the others?"

"Not a lot. I suppose, though, that either Elena or Gretchen Frazier could have been so jealous of the other's relationship with Markham that one of them took it out on him—in the ultimate way."

"The others you met?"

I shrugged. "Greenbaum seems like something of a wimp, but that may be deceptive. As I told you, he and Gretchen may have been fooling around with each other last year, to hear Cortland tell it. If she dumped him to spend more time with Markham, I suppose his male pride could have been bruised to the point that he gave the old war-horse a shove, although that seems somewhat farfetched, I know. If anything, Markham would have wanted to push *Greenbaum* into what you refer to as the abyss. After all, it was Greenbaum who deserted Markham and his political philosophy, and the deserter looks like he's eventually going to get what he seems to want, which is the top job in the department, whenever Schmidt retires.

"Speaking of Schmidt, he chuckles a lot and acts like he's pretty benign. But like with the two women, we're talking jealousy, in this case the professional kind, and I don't know just how much these college types are motivated by envy, although I can guess. One thing sticks with me, however: As long as Markham was around, Schmidt would really only be number two in the Political Science Department, regardless of his title. I don't read him as being able to handle that very well, to say the least."

"And the president, Mr. Potter?" Wolfe asked, making a face.

"I didn't meet him, as I told you, only saw him from across the room. He's slick-looking, photogenic, and from Elena's perspective, pretty shallow and superficial. Could he have given Markham the big push? Sure, why not? The way both Elena and Cortland have described him, he'll do pretty much anything to stay where he is, and lately that's meant trying to keep the very loaded Leander Bach happy. Bach, as we know, didn't have any use for Hale Markham, so . . ."

"Pfui."

"Does that mean 'pfui' as in 'all those Prescott people are disgusting wretches and wretchesses'; or maybe 'pfui' as in 'Potter is a lout'; or perhaps 'pfui' as in 'Leander Bach has no business trying to throw his weight around in an academic community'?"

"You know very well there is no such word as wretchess."

"Yeah, well, it sounds like it ought to be a word, although I personally wouldn't describe either Elena Moreau or Gretchen Frazier as a wretchess. I was merely trying to interpret your 'pfui.'"

"I suggest you abandon interpretation and stay with observation," Wolfe said, watching the foam settle in a newly poured glass of beer.

"Okay, and I have an idea where more observation is needed—Markham's house. I'd like to run back up to Prescott and give it a thorough going-over. I'm sure I can get Cortland to let me in."

"What precisely do you expect to find?"

"I'm not sure, but you know how good I am at combing a place. If there's anything at all there that will help us figure out what happened, I'll find it, even though Markham's been dead for weeks. Besides, this is on my own time and at my expense, remember?"

"Except that you're away from here during office hours, so technically it's *my* time," Wolfe corrected. "Are the germination records up to date?"

"As a matter of fact, yes," I shot back. "As you've heard me say before, the personal computer is a wondrous thing. Aren't you glad we finally got one? And it's practically noiseless, unlike the clattering typewriter that used to irritate you so. As for the time I spend on the Prescott business, I'm keeping a log," I said, pulling a notebook from my center desk drawer. "I'll replace every hour I end up owing you by working evenings and on my days off."

Wolfe considered me through lowered eyelids. "Very well. If I were to say no to this questionable venture, I realize full well that I'd never hear the end of it, and no decision is worth that experience. When will you go?"

"Tomorrow, assuming that I can get hold of Cortland and get into the house. I'll give him a call in the morning and probably leave here well before noon."

"Will you be home for dinner?" It's never difficult to identify Wolfe's priorities.

"Sure, why not? I can't imagine anything keeping me at Prescott longer than a few hours. Although based on an early sampling, I must say that the place has more than its share of beauty, and I don't necessarily mean the kind that has to do with oak trees and river valleys and birds that have three different colors on their wings."

Wolfe sighed, rang for more beer, and picked up his book. I knew enough to shut up while I was more or less ahead.

NINE

The next morning after breakfast, I went to my desk at a few minutes after eight and dialed Cortland's office.

"Yes, Mr. Goodman, he's in," Ms. Auburn-Hair said brightly. "I'll put you through. Hold on."

"Are you alone?" I asked when Cortland picked up the receiver.

"Yes," he said eagerly. I actually think the little guy was warming to the hunt. "I hadn't expected to hear from you again so soon."

"A woman I know tells me unpredictability is among my most endearing traits. I'm calling to find out if I can come up today and have a look through Markham's house."

"Well . . . I *suppose* so." He clearly wasn't thrilled at the notion. "Yes, of course—I don't see why not. The only problem, and it's hardly a big one, is that I'll be away all morning. I only have one class Thursdays, at eight-thirty, and a graduate assistant is taking it for me. I'm departing in about twenty minutes and driving up to Kingston to meet with a state representative about the possibility of his addressing my classes and I probably won't return till around one." He paused, deliberating. "Here's what I can do, though: I've got the key to Hale's house, of course, and I'll leave it in the flowerpot on his front stoop on my way to Kingston."

"That's not a terribly original place," I said.

"Well . . . I suppose you're right, but who else is going to want to get into the house?"

"All right, then—in the pot it is." Cortland gave me the address and the directions to Markham's house.

"Tell me, has anybody been through the place since Markham's death?" I asked.

"No, only I, at least as far as I am aware. And I've just been there twice. Once to get the clothes for . . . you know, for his funeral, and the other time to, uh . . . locate an article he had authored for a scholarly quarterly. He'd completed it, and the quarterly wants to publish it posthumously. I think I told you that Hale has a niece in California, didn't I? Her name is Christina; she says she's going to try to come in the next month or so. I've pretty much left the place alone so she can go through everything. Under the circumstances, though, I see no reason you shouldn't undertake an examination. I haven't any idea whether you'll find anything helpful."

"Neither do I, but I've got to start someplace." I thanked Cortland and he thanked me back. After I hung up, I wrote a note to Wolfe, telling him that I'd be gone most of the day, and put it on his desk blotter. He probably was still attacking breakfast up in his room, and from there he'd go straight to the plant rooms at nine.

This time, the drive north wasn't nearly as pleasant as it had been the day before. A light rain began falling almost as soon as I pulled out of the garage, but before I crossed the George Washington Bridge, it had become a cats-and-dogs number that turned the road into a parking lot. Traffic finally thinned out when I got north of Suffern, but the downpour kept up all the way north, making me glad I'd thought to bring a raincoat.

When I got into Prescott, I pulled off on one side of the town square and got my notes from my pocket. Cortland's directions told me I was no more than three blocks from Markham's house. The rain had let up a little by the time I left the square and entered the streets of the residential area, most of which had big trees lining both sides. Down Cedar, onto Van Buren, one block up Oak, and then down Clinton. Markham's block was a row of two-story white frame houses with shutters and green roofs, the type you're likely to find in small towns all over

New York State and New England. They were set well back from the street. Halfway down the block I found the address—one-seventy-nine—which along with several of its neighbors looked like a prime candidate for a Norman Rockwell painting. All they needed to complete the picture were freckle-faced, redheaded kids wearing tennis shoes, riding bikes, and playing ball in the front yards.

I eased to the curb, killed the engine, and climbed out of the Mercedes. The rain had stopped, and the street was as quiet as a museum. I went up the brick sidewalk and the steps to the door, where, just for the hell of it, I rang the bell. Of course there was no answer, and after waiting for all of thirty seconds, I checked in the flowerpot, where I found nothing but dirt and a long-gone geranium. On a hunch, I picked up the welcome mat, but that cupboard was bare, too.

Now I had a decision to make. Either I could enter by the front way or the back; given that at least one pair of eyes and possibly more were watching the block from behind the starched white curtains of neighboring houses, I figured going in the front was less suspicious, assuming I could get in quickly. I pulled out my ring of skeleton keys and selected one that looked to be a match for the front door's inexpensive, name-brand lock. It fit like Cinderella's slipper, and I whispered a thank-you to Markham for not installing a dead bolt as I pushed the door open.

The place smelled stale, which was hardly surprising, since it had been shut since Markham's death. The small vestibule opened into a larger center hall with a stairway to the second floor. The living room was on the right, the dining room on the left. I turned right, into a spacious room decorated in a style that Lily probably would have called "American Miscellany." I liked it, though. I felt I could get comfortable in any seat in the room, which is at the top of my priority list. There were bookcases on either side of the white brick fireplace, and I thought about tackling them but decided to wait until I'd seen more of the house.

Behind the living room was what probably once had

been a sun porch. Markham had turned it into an office. He hadn't bothered to close it off from the living room, but then, why should he? He was the only person living in the house. It was a good working room, with plenty of natural light, even on this overcast day—windows on three sides, low bookshelves under them, a dark wooden desk that looked like it had been built to withstand a nuclear attack, and a personal computer on a small table next to the desk. The PC was a fairly new model, compatible with the one back at the brownstone. The desktop and the rest of the room looked neat and orderly, but maybe Cortland had done some straightening up when he'd been there. If so, his own office could use a little of the same effort.

I was about to move on in my tour when the doorbell chimed. My first impulse was not to answer it, then I thought I'd better at least have a peek at who might be calling on a dead man. Through the curtains on the living room windows, I saw a second car at the curb behind the Mercedes, and, thinking back, it was at that moment I decided on a course of action. I might have done things differently if Wolfe hadn't been so damn surly about the whole Prescott business, but Wolfe's Wolfe and I'm me, and I did get things to happen. You'll have to be the judge of whether it was done the best way.

I went to the front door, pulled it open, and found myself facing an earnest-looking young man in a police uniform who looked like he was just learning to shave. "Yes, sir," he said, touching the bill of his cap. "Patrolman Nevins, Prescott Police. We got a report someone was here, and we stopped by to check on it. Do you have official business in this house?"

"Yes, I do," I said, giving him a friendly, open smile. I didn't invite him in.

"Do you mind telling me what that business is?" he asked in a polite but firm voice. Young Patrolman Nevins had been trained by the book.

"It doesn't concern the police," I said, still smiling.

He looked uncertain, maybe because the book didn't cover this, and before he could say anything, another cop, closer to my age, waddled around the corner of the house. He obviously had been checking in back. "What's up, Charlie?" the newcomer asked Nevins.

"This gentleman says he has a reason to be here, but doesn't want to tell what it is."

"Oh, yeah?" said the older one. He lumbered up the stairs and stood next to his partner, facing me. His nameplate said Sergeant Amundsen. The insignia on his right arm revealed he was one of Prescott's finest. "You a real-estate man?"

"No," I said, keeping the smile on my face.

"A real talker, huh?" Amundsen hooked his thumbs in his belt and eyed me without affection. He was beefy, probably six-one and two-ten, with a ruddy face that wore a "don't-mess-with-me" expression. "Let's see some iden-tification, please."

I pulled out my wallet and handed Amundsen my driver's and private investigator's licenses. "A private cop, eh?" He scowled. "Okay, Mr. Goodwin, what's the story? Don't try to jerk us around."

"Me? Try to jerk someone around? That's not my style—I'm a straight man, Sergeant. Have been since my Boy Scout days."

"You could have fooled me, Ace. All right, then, let's have it straight, without baloney." Amundsen's blood pressure clearly was headed north.

"I'm here on business for my employer, Nero Wolfe, of New York City, same address as mine. No baloney."

Amundsen raised a bushy eyebrow and looked at young Nevins. "The famous fat man?" He turned back to me. He didn't look impressed. "So what's this *business*?" Wolfe would have said the word "Republican" in the same tone.

I shook my head. "Sorry, you'll have to ask our client, Mr. Walter Cortland."

"A smart guy, huh?" Amundsen sneered. I'd obvi-ously touched a sore spot. "You know, you remind me of a grown-up version of some of those wise-ass fraternity guys over at the university. How did you get in the house?"

"The door was unlocked," I said, holding my smile.

Amundsen used a word that clearly indicated he didn't believe me. "I repeat, what's your business here?" Young Nevins looked at him in awe.

"Mr. Cortland will be back in his office at Prescott University or at his home sometime around one," I told him.

Amundsen looked disgusted. "Charlie, check him to see whether he's taken anything from the house. I'm going in to look around."

Nevins patted me down right there on the stoop, found I had no weapon, and told me to empty my pockets with an enthusiasm that indicated I was the first ultradangerous criminal he'd ever frisked. I took everything out—wallet, card case, car keys, handkerchief, a small penknife, some change, and, of course, the batch of skeleton keys. Nevins looked at the keys as I held them in the palm of one hand. "What are these?" he asked. "Or can I guess?"

I held my noncommittal grin but said nothing. "Ed, better come here," Nevins called into the house. "We got us a problem."

"I knew we had a problem when I laid eyes on this one," Amundsen grumbled as he came back to the stoop. "Now what?"

"These." Triumphantly, Nevins held out the key ring.

Amundsen again mouthed what apparently was his favorite word, then looked at me with an expression I took to be somewhere between frustration and downright dislike. "Now, look, Godwin, why not save everybody a lot of trouble and tell us what's going on?"

"Goodwin," I corrected in an even tone. It was all right for me to alter my name, but I wasn't tickled to have others do it. "Sergeant, I have taken nothing from the house, so there's no burglary—and by the way, you're free to check the car, too. And I've done no damage, as you've just seen, so there's no vandalism."

Amundsen glowered at me, then raised his head, thrusting his chins out. "Illegal entry, not to mention suspicious behavior. This isn't New York City, Goodwin, where people can just barge into other people's houses. We're taking you down to the station."

I shrugged, and after Amundsen slammed the front door shut, making sure it was locked, the three of us walked down the sidewalk. At the sergeant's direction, I unlocked the car and opened the trunk, and he and Nevins checked it out, finding nothing more incriminating than a spare tire in the back and the owner's manual in the glove box. They looked disappointed. "Drive, we'll follow," Amundsen commanded. "Go three blocks on Clinton, take a left on Hudson, and go two blocks. The station is on the right, in the middle of the block, facing the square. Pull into the parking lot behind it. And don't try any cute New York tricks. We're right behind you all the way. On second thought, Patrolman Nevins will ride with you."

"I feel like a desperado," I said to Nevins as we pulled away from the curb. "I'm surprised the sergeant didn't insist on putting the cuffs on me, although it would have made steering a little difficult." Nevins said nothing. He just looked at me as I drove, probably wondering about the types who inhabit that strange and incomprehensible city down the river.

I rolled along at twenty-five miles an hour, with Amundsen two car-lengths behind, his flashers on. The sun had come out, and there were plenty of gawking pedestrians on Hudson Street as our little parade pulled into the lot behind the police station, a one-story brick building with white columns on the front. The whole town seemed to be done in American Colonial.

"You'll probably get a commendation for this, Sergeant," I said to Amundsen as we walked in the back door. "And you, too, son," I added to Nevins. "By any chance is there a wanted poster of me on your bulletin board?"

"Just keep flapping your gums if you want more trouble than you've already got, if that's possible," Amundsen huffed. I started to ask which TV police show he got his dialogue from but checked myself. There was no sense wasting my humor on somebody who wouldn't appreciate it.

Inside, Amundsen steered me to a small, windowless room with three straight-backed chairs and a gray metal table against one wall that had seen better days. "Wait here," he said gruffly. Before I could respond, he stormed out and banged the door behind him. The room had all the cozy ambience of police stations everywhere. The only thing on the eggshell-white walls was a calendar from the local Chrysler-Plymouth dealership with a picture of an Irish Setter and a cute litter of puppies. And the only reading material was a brochure with the catchy headline "Ten Tips on How to Keep Your House Safe from Burglars." My watch told me it was eleven-thirteen as I started in learning how to make my house a burglarproof fortress.

Seven minutes and four tips later, the door opened and a tall, thin specimen wearing a brown suit and with more hair above his eyes than on top of his head came in, shut the door hard, and looked down at me. His eyes were little and mean. "Mr. Goodwin, I'm Lieutenant Powers. Sergeant Amundsen has filled me in on what happened at Professor Markham's house. He also told me you had nothing to say. You'll talk to me."

I glanced up, trying my best to look bored, which wasn't hard. "What am I charged with, Lieutenant?"

"Don't get smart with me." Like Amundsen, he liked to sneer. Must be something they teach them at the academy. "Remember, you're not in New York City now."

"I've been reminded of that already today," I said lightly. I was beginning to know how Clint Eastwood feels in a new town. "You folks seem to have a real complex about New York. Am I being held without a charge?"

"Listen, goddamn it, if we want to book you, we'll have no problem doing it. Breaking and entering, for starters. Now are you going to tell me what you were doing in Professor Markham's house?"

"Well, I guess you've bullied it out of me," I answered. "As I told Sergeant Amundsen, my employer, Nero Wolfe, and I have a client named Walter Cortland, of whom you may have heard. He's a professor at the university, and he thinks Hale Markham was murdered. He hired us to confirm—or refute—his contention."

"Yeah, Ed mentioned that damned Cortland." Powers actually snarled. "I might have known. What a pain-in-the—oh, the hell with it. Listen, Einstein, if you're working for that whiny pest, how come you didn't just get a key to Markham's place from him, huh?" He looked down at me with a smirk and I wondered if, like his New York Police counterpart, Lieutenant Rowcliff, he stuttered when he lost control. It was tempting to find out, but probably not worth the effort.

"He went up to Kingston for the morning and he forgot to leave me the key, Lieutenant, it's as simple as that. Honest. Call him—he can tell you. He's supposed to be back by about one."

Powers fired more questions at me, but I got stubborn and folded my arms, staring straight ahead. After about half a minute, he realized we'd exhausted the conversation and stalked out, slamming the door harder than Amundsen had. I clearly was making no friends in Prescott.

Five minutes later the door opened and a square-faced, gray-haired, lanky number in a white uniform shirt and black tie pushed in. The nameplate on his pocket read HOBSON. "Mr. Goodwin," he said curtly, "I am Carl Hobson, chief of police here in Prescott, and I'm here to find out precisely what the hell's going on." He enunciated each word, probably to underscore to me that, unlike the others I'd talked to, he *really* meant business.

I looked up at him. "Am I being charged?" I asked quietly.

"Maybe you don't realize it, but you're in a lot of trouble, mister," he said, sounding like a poor imitation of James Cagney in *Mr. Roberts*. The guy must be a scream at a party. "We've already been around the course with Walter Cortland and his crazy notions about murder. The last thing we need is somebody waltzing in here from—"

"New York?" I offered.

He looked at me coldly with his light blue eyes and continued without missing a beat. "—who thinks he's going to create headlines by trying to invent a murder. For your information, there hasn't been a homicide in this community in twenty-seven years, and it's despicable to think that someone like yourself and your publicity-hungry boss would take advantage of poor Professor Cortland's grief over losing his friend just to generate a case—and notoriety—for yourselves."

"I think you should talk to Mr. Cortland," I said in an even, unemotional tone. I'd been so deadpan for the last few hours I was beginning to worry it might become a permanent condition. "He should be back in town about one o'clock."

"You're damn right I'll talk to him, mister," Hobson said, his voice rising a notch. His color did the same. "And for your sake, you'd better hope he says the right things. You're under arrest."

"The charge?"

"Illegal entry," he spat. "Follow me."

And damned if they didn't book me. They took my keys, wallet, and other possessions and gave me a receipt for them. A polite sergeant named Pierce filled out the paperwork, set my bond at five hundred dollars, and asked me if I wanted to call an attorney.

"Thanks anyway," I told him with a smile, "but I'm compiling a guide to jails in the eastern United States, and this will give me another entry—under the heading 'Hamlets and Backwaters I Have Known.'" He looked up from the desk with a puzzled expression, then shrugged and somewhat apologetically escorted me down a hall to one of four small cells, none of which was occupied. "Our main customers are from the university," Pierce said cheerfully, "usually the fraternity boys who get carried away at their parties and . . . you know."

"I can guess," I said as he held the door of one of the cells, gesturing me in. It was small but reasonably clean, with the standard fixtures—bunk, toilet, washstand, matching wooden table and chair—and actually had a window that looked out on the parking lot, where I could at least keep watch over the Mercedes.

"Pardon me, Sergeant," I said as he started to swing the barred door shut, "but would there by any chance be a newspaper handy that I could look at?"

"I'll check, sir," he said, and less than a minute later he was back with that day's *Albany Times-Union*. After thanking him profusely, I read the whole thing through twice, including the piece on how Prescott was an eighteen-point underdog against Syracuse in Saturday's game. They'll be lucky to come that close, I thought as I tossed the paper aside, then settled back on the bunk. Time: twelve-forty-nine.

A few minutes later, I awoke from the clank of the cell door opening and figured my watch must be lying. The face claimed it was three-ten, but of course that had to be a mistake. Sergeant Pierce had stepped into the cell, telling me to follow him.

"First, what time is it?" I asked, shaking myself.

"Uh, three-eleven," he said with a lopsided smile. "Guess you flaked out. Maybe you can put in that book of yours that our bunks are comfortable, huh? You're wanted in the old man's office." Whistling, he led the way down a hall toward the front of the building, where I hadn't yet been. He rapped his knuckles lightly on a mahogany door with a polished metal nameplate that said CHIEF CARL W. HOBSON, then turned the knob and eased it open.

The chief, still wearing his uniform shirt and tie and a scowl, sat behind a large wooden desk in a nicely carpeted office. He glared at me as Pierce ushered me in. Seated off to his right, in a chair far too small for him, also glaring, was Nero Wolfe.

TEN

Wolfe told me later with more than a little satisfaction that my mouth dropped open when I walked in. I didn't believe him when he said it and I don't believe him now, but in truth, he was about the last person I expected to find in Prescott's police station. In those first few seconds after I saw him, all I could think about was how in the hell he'd gotten there. It must have been Saul, I said to myself—he's the only person besides myself that Wolfe's ever trusted as his driver.

The gregarious Lieutenant Powers swaggered in seconds after I did, and he and I sat in the two other chairs that formed the rest of the arc in front of the elaborately carved mahogany desk of Carl W. Hobson, a man who obviously enjoyed the trappings of office. I took the seat farthest from Wolfe, who looked like he wanted to take a bite out of someone.

Hobson didn't exactly appear to be at peace with the world himself. He stared at Powers for several seconds, then turned his headlights on me. "Goodwin," he snarled. I was going to congratulate him on remembering my name more than three hours after meeting me, but before I could get the words out, he brought his palm down hard on the desk, presumably for effect. He needed to take lessons from Wolfe on desk pounding, though; his technique was all wrong.

"Okay, wise guy," Hobson said to me with another snarl. "Your boss is here now, wanting to get you out.

Suppose you fill us in on just what you were doing in Markham's house."

"Do I unload?" I asked, looking across at Wolfe, whom I knew was suffering for about six reasons, not the least of which was the chair he'd somehow shoehorned himself into. He nodded grimly.

"All right," I said, leaning back and crossing one leg over the other. "I've told you some of this already: A Prescott professor named Walter Cortland called us in New York on Monday . . ." I proceeded to give them a narrative, from Cortland's contention that Markham had been bumped off that cliff to my trip to the campus the day before, including my visits to the classes and the bottom of the Gash, and lunch with the various faculty members. I did some editing, though, leaving out the coffee with Gretchen Frazier and the session in Elena Moreau's office. As I talked, I watched Hobson's expression go from dour to incredulous to unbelieving. Powers shook his head a lot, and Wolfe just went on looking grumpy. I finished by saying that Cortland was supposed to have left me the key to Markham's place so I could have a look around, but when it wasn't there, I let myself in. "And that's when your boys came along," I said to the chief, lacing my hands behind my head.

"This is ridiculous!" Hobson growled, running a hand through his hair. "My men were at the location within minutes after the professor's body was found. There was no indication he'd been pushed or that there was a struggle. The medical report showed he died of a broken neck from the fall," he snapped, yanking a sheet from a manila folder on his desk. "I'll tell you what I think," he said, leaning on his elbows and his vowels. "I think you New York hotshots figure you can throw your weight around up here in what you like to call 'the sticks,' trying to generate some easy business for yourselves. Well, I'll tell you both," he went on, waving a bony and none-too-clean finger at us, "you're not welcome here, not for a minute. And you—what have you got to say for yourself?" he asked, turning to Wolfe. "You've barely spoken a word since you walked in here."

Wolfe tried to adjust himself in the chair, a physical impossibility. I was trying to recall when someone last addressed Wolfe as "you" and lived to tell about it.

"You've charged Mr. Goodwin with breaking and entering," he intoned without emotion.

"That's right, good guess." The chief nodded and stuck out his lower lip. He was obviously pleased with himself.

"It is *not* a guess," Wolfe growled. "I know what the charge is because Mr. Cortland told me on the telephone at a few minutes after one. He also informed me that one of your minions, this gentleman here"—he gestured toward Powers with an almost imperceptible tilt of the head—"had called him shortly after he returned home from Kingston to tell him of Mr. Goodwin's booking. When Mr. Cortland attempted to explain that he had given Mr. Goodwin express permission to go through the house, but that he had forgotten to leave the key in a prearranged place, your officer had no interest in what he was saying and rudely cut him off."

"Hey, wait a minute, I—"

"Lloyd, I'll handle this." The chief stifled Powers with a karate-chop motion of his hand. "Mr. Wolfe, you should know that from the day Professor Markham's body was found, Cortland has been driving us nuts about this, claiming it was murder. He's probably called here a half-dozen times, maybe more, insisting we look further into the death. But, and I stress this, he has never, not once, come up with a shred of evidence to substantiate his allegations." He leaned back and stuck out the lower lip again.

"So in a fit of pique, both to spite Mr. Cortland and to show the New Yorkers who's boss in your realm, you ignored him and jailed Mr. Goodwin. This despite the insistence of Mr. Cortland—the executor of the Markham estate—that he had approved in advance Mr. Goodwin's entry into the house."

"Cortland may have approved it in advance, but nobody bothered to tell us," Hobson protested. The red in his cheeks was turning to purple. "And furthermore, how were my men supposed to know Goodwin was legitimate? After all, he got in with one of that dandy set of keys he carries. In my book—and in this town—that's pretty damn suspicious behavior, to say the least."

"I'll concede that Mr. Goodwin on occasion uses questionable judgment and tactics," Wolfe said. "But you know now that his entry into the house, however unorthodox, was made with prior approval of an authorized party, and that no damage was done to its interior. I suggest that to save yourselves possible embarrassment later, you drop the matter at this point."

He squeezed himself out of the chair with sublime effort, rose, and motioned me to do the same, which I did. "Good day, sir," he said.

"Wait a minute," Hobson rasped. "You—"

"No, *you* wait a minute, sir," Wolfe fired back in a voice that would have frozen a hot toddy. "Since you seem to harbor animus toward anyone from Manhattan, you should be more than happy to see Mr. Goodwin and me leave. And we are pleased to accommodate you."

Hobson was standing now, too, his puss as colorful as a slice of Rusterman's rare prime rib. The guy was trying to figure out how to keep from losing face, especially with his second-in-command in the room.

"You know, Goodwin is still in custody," he barked. "We can keep him from leaving."

Wolfe, who had made it almost to the door, turned slowly and fixed his gaze on the chief. "I don't doubt that for a moment," he said, "but such an action would be so ill-advised as to be classed as Brobdingnagian folly. I strongly suggest you consider alternatives."

Hobson took a couple of deep breaths. You can't blame him—Brobdingnagian throws me, too. "All right," he said finally, in a thin voice, as if making a major concession, "I'll do this—I'll release Goodwin with the understanding that if he is needed for questioning, you will make him available to this department or to the district attorney's office."

"I assume," Wolfe said, holding fast at the door, "that such questioning would likely relate to a felony, perhaps a capital crime, to merit Mr. Goodwin's return here. I am unaware that you feel a crime of such magnitude has taken place."

I could have strangled Wolfe. Hobson's expression clearly reflected his puzzlement, and for a moment, I thought he might renege on his offer. But he was between the proverbial rock and hard place. After another deep breath, the chief abandoned his attempt to save face and told us both to get the hell out.

"And the charge is dropped?" Wolfe persisted, still not budging.

"Yes, dammit," Hobson said, his face now the color of a wedge of watermelon. "Goodwin can pick up his belongings at the front desk!"

With that, Wolfe marched out, with me two paces behind. He turned right and went into the entrance hall, where Saul Panzer was sitting in a straight-backed metal chair reading a dog-eared copy of the bathing-suit issue of *Sports Illustrated*, which looked like it was missing more than a few pages. "Saul, we're going," Wolfe announced, and the two of them stood waiting as I retrieved my pocketload of possessions, including the skeleton keys. I made a big deal out of checking to make sure everything was there, then signed the sheet Pierce slipped across the desk at me and thanked him. Still whistling, Pierce winked.

Saul, who as usual looked like he could use a shave, nodded and gave me a thumbs-up as he popped his flat cap on and set it at a rakish angle. "Did you find out about rooms?" Wolfe asked him when we were on the sidewalk in front of the police station.

"Yep. Best place around, no contest, is the Prescott Inn, which is just off the campus. I've reserved rooms for both you and Archie there tonight. I'm told the food's first-rate, too, although with what you're used to, there's a better-than-even chance that it may not measure up."

"Satisfactory," Wolfe said. As far as he's concerned, Saul Panzer can do no wrong, and I'd have to second that. Saul isn't impressive to look at, given a face that's all nose, stooped shoulders that make him seem even shorter than he is, and a wardrobe the Salvation Army would reject for its resale stores. But he's far and away the finest street operative in Manhattan, and probably the United States, which is why Wolfe always calls on him when we need a tailing job or a casing job or hard-to-get information about anyone from a two-bit thief to a corporation president.

"Pretty fancy wheels," I said to Saul, tapping the fender of the forest-green Lincoln Town Car parked at the curb. "You two drive up in this?"

Saul shrugged. "It seemed like the best the rental place had, and it handles okay. Where's the Mercedes, in back?"

I said it was and told Wolfe to wait while I brought it around. As I walked away, Wolfe was thanking Saul for the chauffeuring job and wishing him a good drive back to New York. And he meant it; to Wolfe, any drive, regardless of length, is a risky venture at best, which I knew was why he had decided on staying the night in Prescott. Anything was preferable to two seventy-five-mile drives in the same day.

I pulled up in front of the station. Wolfe was indeed a vision, wearing his gray overcoat and black homburg and holding tightly to his redthorn walking stick. I was sorry more of the citizenry of Prescott wasn't around to appreciate this historic sight: the world's greatest private detective standing on a sidewalk in a small town in upstate New York. And glowering.

As I eased to the curb, Saul opened the back door for Wolfe, then closed it behind him and put his suitcase and my smaller overnight bag on the front seat next to me. "Archie, Fritz packed a change of clothes for you and put your shaving kit in there, too," Saul said.

"Bless him. And bless you, too, my son," I told him and saluted. Pulling away, I could see Saul in my rearview mirror thumbing his nose at me and grinning from sideburn to sideburn.

"I suppose you'd like to go straight to the Prescott Inn?" I asked Wolfe.

"Confound it, yes!" he grumbled as he adjusted

himself and gripped the passenger strap as if it were a lifeline thrown to a drowning man. I followed the directions that Saul had scratched on a sheet of paper, and three minutes later, we were in front of a two-story, American Colonial—what else?—mansion on a tree-lined street just outside the town's business district and within sight of the very building where Cortland had his office.

"Looks nice," I observed, and was rewarded with a grunt from the back seat, where Wolfe was still clutching the strap even though I had stopped the car. As far as he's concerned, you simply can't be too careful when you're traveling, and for once, I had to agree.

ELEVEN

The Prescott Inn was first-rate, all right. With a minimum of fuss, I got Wolfe settled in his room, which turned out to be a suite—bedroom and sitting room—both decorated of course in Early American. And the sitting room had a chair that came reasonably close to accommodating Wolfe's dimensions, which is saying something. Saul had done his job, as usual. My room was next door, and while it would never be mistaken for a suite, it was far from shabby itself.

"Okay," I told Wolfe after I'd unpacked his stuff and put it away. "I know you're sore as hell about being here, and you're sore at me for getting you here. In fact, you're sore about this whole damn situation. But to show my good faith, I'm going to order you beer from room service—it's on me."

He sat and pouted in the big chair while I called down and asked the voice at the other end to have two bottles of Remmers sent up for him and milk for me. Then I took a chair facing him. "Are you going to talk, or just sit there and let me prattle on?"

"Pah. That man was hysterical."

"Who?"

"Mr. Cortland, of course. When he telephoned me, he was in a dither, to the point where he neglected to use any of his polysyllabic vocabulary. He reported that the police had told him you were being held but refused to give him any further information. To hear his histrionics, one would have thought you were only minutes from an appointment with the guillotine. I contemplated calling the Prescott police myself, but chose instead, with Saul's assistance, to beard them in their den." He leaned back and closed his eyes, looking insufferably smug, as if to say that I, the man of action, needed him, the original stay-at-home, to enter the arena and put things right.

"I'm genuinely touched that you'd make this trek, and just to get me out of a hole at that," I said.

The corner of his mouth twitched. "Need I remind you, Archie, that this contretemps began with high-sounding pronouncements about how you were investigating Mr. Markham's murder at your own expense, and on your own time. I might have known that—"

I was saved from this further onslaught of smugness by the bell, or rather, the bellhop. He was at the door, all five-feet-four of him, with a pencil-thin mustache, black shoe-polished hair parted in the middle, and a smile that made Vanna White look like a mope by comparison. So much for insignificant details; the important fact was that he had two chilled bottles of Wolfe's favorite beer, Remmers, along with a pilsner glass, and my milk. I paid him, added a tip that made the smile even wider, and took the tray, setting it on the end table at Wolfe's left.

"Interesting historical fact: This is the oldest college in New York State," I said as he poured beer and studied the settling foam.

"University," he corrected, looking unimpressed. "We should call Mr. Cortland. What time is it?"

"Four-oh-five. You want me to try him now?"

"Later. Have you eaten since breakfast?"

"Negative. Funny, I was just thinking about my stomach. It's a little early for dinner, though. I can stand to wait a couple of hours. Did you have something before you left?"

"Barely." Wolfe winced at the memory. "Mr. Cortland's frenzied call came just as I was finishing lunch."

"Gulping down your food is rough on the digestive system," I sympathized. "Do you want dinner in the dining room, or should I have it brought up here?"

"Here," Wolfe said quietly. He obviously was preparing for the worst. To him, a meal away from Fritz is the next thing to a sentence on Devil's Island.

"Well, I assume you'd like to start thinking about it anyway. Try the room service menu," I said, taking it from the desk and handing it across. "What's the program?"

Wolfe sucked in slightly more than a bushel of air and let it out slowly. "I want to see Mr. Cortland—preferably before dinner."

"Any other instructions?"

"Not at the moment," he said airily, opening the menu.

"Okay, I'll be next door." I got up to go, and his eyes stayed on the menu, one of his ways of telling me he didn't particularly care what I did, other than reaching Cortland. In my room, I dialed the professor at home, then at the office; no answer at either place. I dropped onto the bed and closed my eyes; after all, I was newly released from incarceration and needed a period of readjustment to society, to say nothing of a recharging of my batteries. When I opened my eyes, it was a few ticks before five. I got up and opened my overnight bag. Fritz had done a terrific packing job, including everything I could possibly need for a stay of three or four days. I briefly considered calling home to thank him, but scratched the idea; Fritz always frets when Wolfe is away from home and would probably strafe me with questions about how he felt, whether he was getting enough to eat, whether he was dressing warmly enough, and so on. I could do without that just now.

I washed up and tried Cortland at home again, this time with success. "I'm over at the Prescott Inn," I announced. "So is Wolfe."

"Oh? You've been released?" He sounded surprised.

"Yes. What happened to that damn key that you were supposed to leave in the flowerpot?"

"Oh, Mr. Goodwin, I'm so chagrined," he said. "In my hurry to leave for Kingston—I'm afraid I was running late as usual—I simply forgot. I don't know what to say—"

"Say you'll never do it again, cross your heart. Their dungeon is horrible, but somehow I survived it all. That's all in the past, though. Mr. Wolfe would like to see you here. I strongly suggest that you come as fast as you can."

Cortland said he'd make it fifteen minutes, which meant that if Wolfe didn't prolong the meeting, he could still have his dinner at the usual time—or even earlier, if he was of a mind. I mention this because his stomach in large measure—no pun intended—dictates his actions. I gave myself nine-to-two odds that his conversation with Cortland would take no more than an hour and probably less. I ran a comb through my hair and dialed Wolfe's suite. He answered on the third ring. "Yes?" His tone was the same one I get when I interrupt him during one of his sessions in the plant rooms.

"Mr. Cortland will be over in less than ten minutes now, or so he promises. Do you want me to order dinner before he gets here and have it brought up at, say, seven?"

There was a five-second pause, followed by a deep breath, intended to represent suffering. "Yes. I'll have the endive salad, the chicken and dumplings, the strawberries Romanoff, and coffee." From his tone, it was obvious he wasn't about to bet his house in Cairo on the abilities of the folks manning the kitchen. "Also, Archie, have more beer brought up now, and something for you and Mr. Cortland as well."

Having been thus directed, I called downstairs and gave them two identical dinner orders—I liked the sound of Wolfe's choices. I also asked them to send up more beer and a bottle of their highest-priced Scotch, along with soda. I didn't know anything for sure about Cortland's preferences, but he seemed like a Scotch drinker. If I happened to be wrong, there was always room service, we could easily become their best customers.

After I got off the phone, I looked in the mirror, straightened my tie, and went down the hall to Wolfe's door, knocking once and pronouncing my name. He grunted and I let myself in with the key. He was right where I'd left him in the big chair, except now he had a new book, *A History of Venice*, by John Julius Norwich.

"Beer's on the way," I told him. "And so, as you know, is Cortland. Are you ready for him?" My answer was a glare, which lasted all of three seconds before he returned to his book. The sawed-off waiter with the mustache, the smile, and the libations beat the professor to our room, only by a minute or so. Wolfe had his beer and I was unscrewing the cap on the Scotch when the knock came. I went to the door and cracked it, bracing it with one foot, which turned out to be unnecessary. The man in the hall appeared about as likely as Woody Allen to bull his way into a room.

"Enter," I told Cortland, who blinked, gave a whispered hello, and cautiously stepped in, squaring his shoulders. He was wearing a nicely cut light gray suit, a great improvement over those ridiculous rainbow sportcoats. "Please sit down, Mr. Cortland," Wolfe rumbled, gesturing toward the upholstered chair that I'd positioned facing him. "Will you have something to drink?"

"Scotch, please—with soda if you've got it." Score one for my character analysis. I stirred Scotch-and-sodas for Cortland and myself while Wolfe poured the first of three bottles of Remmers that were lined up like soldiers at parade rest on the table. I handed our guest his drink, pulled up a straight-backed chair for myself, and flipped my notebook open.

"Sir," Wolfe said after taking a healthy swallow of beer, "as I believe you know, the Prescott police now are aware you have engaged me to investigate Mr. Markham's death. Under the circumstances, Mr. Goodwin had very little alternative but to divulge our role to them. How do you feel about this?"

Cortland sipped Scotch and set his glass down gingerly. "It was going to come out eventually," he said, shrugging.

"It was indeed. Now that I'm here," Wolfe said, allowing himself an expression that showed his near-misery, "I would like to talk to several people, preferably in a group. And it would be helpful if you could orchestrate this."

Cortland fidgeted. As I watched him, I realized he didn't have any idea how unusual it was for Wolfe to be unleashed on the world. You'd better not blow this opportunity, buddy, I thought, either for your sake or for our almighty and most honorable bank balance.

"Well, I suppose I can at least ask," the professor said, bobbing his head and clearing his throat. "I think I know who you want to engage in conversation, and when they see Mr. Goodwin, they'll realize I wasn't being totally forthright with them the first time he paid a visit. You know, the false name and all." He stared glumly into his Scotch, no doubt wondering how the coming events would affect his academic reputation.

"As you said yourself, it was going to come out anyway."

"True. You'll want to see . . ."

"Messrs. Schmidt, Greenbaum, and Potter, and the two women, Elena Moreau and Gretchen Frazier," Wolfe said, turning a hand over.

"When would you want them here?"

"After dinner would be ideal, at nine o'clock. If any are unable to be present, we could see them individually tomorrow, but only in the morning. Mr. Goodwin and I will be leaving before midday. I can afford no more time away from home."

"And if none want to come?"

"You might suggest that if I leave here without seeing them, my recourse will be to share my suspicions with journalists in New York who *will* be interested in talking to me."

"You're asking a lot on short notice," Cortland protested with a squeak.

"Mr. Cortland, it is a rare occurrence—and a great inconvenience—for me to leave my home for any reason, and when I do, I ask the indulgence of others. After all, I have in effect indulged *you* by coming here. You are welcome to use this telephone to make the requisite calls." Wolfe was laying it on thick, which didn't bother me at all.

Besides, his little speech had told me when we'd be checking out of Prescott, which was more than I had known before.

"Thank you, but I'll use the instrument at home," Cortland said primly. "What should I say?"

Wolfe scowled. "Try the truth. Tell them you think Mr. Markham was murdered and that you have engaged me to ferret out the murderer. Tell them also that I've asked to talk to a number of people who knew Mr. Markham. And suggest that anyone who does not come to see me will be suspect. You might choose to add as an incentive that if they do not come to this room, Mr. Goodwin will pay calls on the recalcitrants. One more thing: Say that if transportation is a problem, Mr. Goodwin will drive any one of them to and from here." I've always been impressed at how free Wolfe is with my time and duties.

Cortland still had a troubled look as he drained his drink. "I'm honestly not sure if I can get them— particularly Potter and Schmidt."

"But you can try," Wolfe insisted coolly. "Mr. Goodwin and I will await your report. One more question, sir: Why did you neglect to mention in your conversations with us that Mr. Markham suffered from dizzy spells?"

The professor wrinkled his brow and shook his head. "What dizzy spells? Hale never had anything like that. The man was a rock."

"Not according to Mrs. Moreau."

"Mr. Wolfe, I was Hale's closest friend—his confidant. If he had had attacks of dizziness, I most certainly would have been cognizant of it," Cortland said in an offended tone. "I don't know what Elena thinks she's up to, but this is manifestly nonsense!"

"Very well," Wolfe said, expressionless. "Mr. Goodwin will see you to the door."

Cortland's expression alternated between anger and confusion as he rose to leave. He briefly muttered about Elena's motives, then switched to grumbling about how difficult he thought his calling assignment was, but he might as well have had a tree as his listener. Wolfe had opened his book, a clear signal the audience was over. I escorted Cortland to the hall, arming him with a pep talk about how much faith both of us had in him. Closing the door, I turned to Wolfe.

"I've got to agree with our client," I said. "I'm not sure he'll be able to get many of them."

He looked up peevishly. "The moment has arrived for Mr. Cortland to do a little work. What time is it?"

"Six-ten. Why?"

Wolfe's frown deepened, but he said nothing, returning to his book. I knew he was hungry and had hoped it was nearer dinnertime. Even though he was in alien territory, miles from the kitchen, larder, and talents of Fritz Brenner, he and his stomach were primed for dinner. For that matter, so was I.

TWELVE

As it turned out, the dinner merited our anticipation. Wolfe pronounced the chicken and dumplings "more than adequate," and I had to agree, scoring them at least a high B on my own scale, which is saying something, given my years dining on the creations of Fritz Brenner. Wolfe was anchored in his chair for the meal, which got wheeled in on a tablecloth-covered cart at precisely seven o'clock by none other than our mustachioed and minuscule dandy of a waiter, whom I rewarded with a finif, if only to see just how wide that grin could stretch. I pulled one of the straight-backed chairs up to the cart and mainly chewed and listened while Wolfe expounded on why terms of members of the House of Representatives should be extended from two years to four. He was surprisingly amiable, given that I'd uprooted him from home and routine and that he would soon be spending the night in a bed designed for mortals of standard proportions. His mood dived into the basement fast, though, when a call came from Cortland that indicated he would now have to do something to earn his fee.

I listened on the bedroom extension while the professor reported to Wolfe that, much to his astonishment, he had connected with all five subjects, and that three of them—Schmidt, Greenbaum, and Elena Moreau—had agreed to see Wolfe that night at nine. Potter and Gretchen Frazier claimed previous engagements, although the president, after much grumpling, said he would come at nine-thirty the next morning, while Gretchen was set for eleven.

"I should tell you that they weren't exactly elated, though." Cortland sounded none too pleased himself. "Particularly Schmidt and Greenbaum. The only way I sold Orville was to tell him that Ted and Elena already had agreed to see you. And then there was Potter: He took umbrage at first and voiced the opinion that the entire notion of murder was ridiculous. When I informed him several of the faculty had already agreed to come to your room, he retreated and said he would talk to you in his office tomorrow. My response was that you were not prepared to leave the Inn under any circumstances, and he snorted and said okay, he'd humor you. I think his primary concern is about bad publicity for the school."

"Undoubtedly. How did the women react?"

"Elena didn't seem terribly surprised for some reason. At least she didn't fight the idea, although she complained that she was in the middle of grading papers. As far as the Frazier girl, she sounded shocked—and a little frightened, too, I'd have to say."

"Very well," Wolfe said. "You probably will hear from Mr. Goodwin sometime tomorrow."

"You don't want me to be there when you talk to the others?"

"Not necessary," Wolfe said curtly, which caused a relieved sigh on the other end.

"You have to admit he did pretty well," I said as I walked back to where Wolfe was polishing off the last of the strawberries Romanoff. "Adequate" was all I got out of him, though, before he told me to call for more beer and other liquid reinforcements for our next guests. I ordered four bottles of Remmers this time, plus a bottle each of bourbon and gin and a good white wine, plus a variety of mixes, just to be on the safe side. If the faculty wanted anything more exotic, they'd have to find it elsewhere.

Our beaming waiter, smelling still another tip, wheeled in a cart loaded with bottles, ice, and glasses at eight-forty-three, giving me time to set up a makeshift bar on the buffet in one corner of the room. Wolfe had returned to his book after pouring one of the two bottles of beer I had set on the end table next to him. I moved the sofa and one upholstered chair into position facing him—he doesn't like to crane his neck—and positioned a chair for myself off to the left where I could keep an eye on all their faces.

When a knock came at nine-oh-six, I opened the door a crack on three less-than-happy faces. "Come in, please," I said, trying to make it sound hospitable.

"Mr. Goodwin, isn't it? Or should I say *Goodman*?" The smile on Schmidt's round face didn't match his testy tone. The lanky Greenbaum stuck out a long jaw and brushed by me, while Elena Moreau, looking every bit as chic as she had the day before, fixed me with narrowed eyes. She gave herself away, though, when the right corner of her mouth turned up, and I responded with a wink as she moved into the room.

"Well, we're here, but I'm damned if I know why we should be," Schmidt declared to Wolfe as if he were beginning to lecture a hall full of freshmen. "If what Walter told us on the phone is true—"

"Mr. Schmidt, if you please," Wolfe interrupted, getting as comfortable as his chair allowed, "hear me out and perhaps in our discussions the truth will present itself. Mrs. Moreau. Mr. Greenbaum." He dipped his head a fraction of an inch to each of them. "Please be seated. I prefer to have others at eye level. Mr. Goodwin will be happy to serve refreshments. As you can see, I'm having beer."

"We know him as Arnold Goodman," Greenbaum brayed, easing into a spot on the sofa next to Elena, while Schmidt dropped into the armchair. "And nothing for me—I don't intend to stay long. I don't think any of us do." Schmidt, who had obviously nominated himself as spokesman for the trio, wasn't about to get upstaged and turned to Greenbaum, who immediately shut up.

"Mr. Wolfe," Schmidt said, planting his elbows on the chair arms, "we came tonight because a colleague asked us to. We met down in the lobby and decided we would hear you out, despite your high-handed tactic of summoning us as if we were suppliants being called before a feudal lord. I will have bourbon on the rocks. Elena?"

"White wine, please," she said, glancing my way with the beginnings of a real smile.

"Better than a feudal lord likely would have offered suppliants," Wolfe observed as I set the drinks on end tables next to Schmidt and Elena. Greenbaum folded his arms over his chest and stuck out that chin again. It was a tempting target.

"I appreciate the time you have taken, and I promise not to prolong the evening unnecessarily," Wolfe said without a trace of sarcasm. "As Mr. Cortland told each of you on the telephone, Mr. Goodwin and I are here to determine whether your former colleague, Hale Markham, fell to his death accidentally or was pushed."

"Or killed himself?" Elena Moreau queried, raising her beautifully shaped eyebrows. "As ludicrous as it sounds, that possibility has been suggested." That zinger was meant for me.

"A possibility as well," Wolfe conceded.

"I say nonsense—to *both* murder and suicide!" Schmidt barked, slapping a palm on his knee. "Nobody had any reason to kill Hale, and he was far too enamored of himself to commit suicide."

"Really, Orville, aren't we getting a bit nasty?" Elena said, turning toward him with anger in her voice and in her large, dark eyes.

"Well, it's true, Elena. I know you were friends—good friends—and I respect that, whatever I may have thought of Hale personally. But even you would have to agree that the man had an ego the size of the Himalayas."

She continued glaring at him and he finally looked away, his chubby cheeks an even rosier shade than usual. "Mr. Wolfe," she said, "I'd be interested—I think we all would—in hearing precisely why you believe Hale was murdered."

"I haven't said I believe he was murdered, madam. I said I am here to determine *whether* he was."

"Hah! It sounds to me like you're fishing for business," Greenbaum snapped, aiming his chin at Wolfe again.

"I assure you, sir, that I do not have to fish for business, as you put it. The fish come to me—they always have. Am I correct in stating that none of you thinks there was the slightest possibility Mr. Markham's death was not accidental?" He fixed his eyes on each of the three in turn, ending with Elena.

They all nodded and murmured yesses. "Mrs. Moreau," Wolfe said, keeping his attention on her, "did you not tell Mr. Goodwin that Hale Markham had suffered fainting spells in recent months?"

"What kind of nonsense is that?" It was Schmidt, his litmus-paper face reddening again. "Whatever else Hale may have been, he sure as hell wasn't feeble or faintish."

"If you please, sir." Wolfe dismissed him with a glance and turned back to Elena.

"It—the fainting, that is—happened twice when he was with me, once walking across campus, the other time outside a restaurant."

"You are suggesting Mr. Markham had a fainting spell as he walked near the edge of the Gash?" Wolfe asked.

"Not necessarily—you brought the subject up. But it's certainly a possible explanation."

"Was Mr. Markham without enemies?"

Elena shrugged. "I suppose we all have enemies, if you want to call them that. Especially someone as strong-minded and outspoken as Hale. But there's a world of difference between an enemy and a murderer."

"Granted. Who would you identify as his enemies?"

Elena took a deep breath and then a sip of her wine, obviously buying time. "Well—"

"See here!" Schmidt jerked in his chair. "We're not going to sit still for this high-handed inquisition. We—"

"Sir, Mrs. Moreau is speaking," Wolfe shot back. "If she does not choose to reply, she is perfectly capable of conveying that information. Madam?"

"All right," she said, sitting up straight on the sofa

and uncrossing her legs, "I'll tell you who *Hale* saw as his enemies." She took another deep breath to collect herself.

"You've heard of Leander Bach, of course. He and Hale loathed each other—I guess that's pretty much public knowledge."

"And the reason for their mutual animus?"

"Political philosophy, basically. Bach doesn't have a degree, but he did go to school for a year way back when—and at Prescott, of all places. He has said publicly that he still feels a loyalty to the university, and in the last few months, there had been a lot of talk about the likelihood of his giving money—a pile of money—to Prescott. When that talk began, Hale made some caustic remarks in one of his classes about Bach's left-wing leanings and his well-publicized visits to the Soviet Union. Somebody from the campus paper was in the class, and the paper sent a reporter to see Hale, who repeated it all and more in an interview that they printed on page one with a big headline. Hale really blasted Bach—called him a 'mushy-headed neo-Marxist' and said the university could do very nicely without his money. You can imagine the flak that caused."

"How did Mr. Bach react?"

"Violently. Needless to say, the campus paper smelled a wonderful brawl and went to him for reaction. Bach claimed that as long as Hale was on the Prescott faculty, he'd find more deserving places to give his money. He called Hale a Neanderthal, among other things."

"I'd call Hale mainly stupid for having looked a gift horse in the mouth," Greenbaum grumbled. Wolfe glared at him and then turned back to Elena. "That decision of course made your president unhappy."

"Potter? God, yes, the man was beside himself. Hale told me later that Keith summoned him to his office and went into a tantrum. He called Hale a traitor to the university. Apparently it was quite a spectacle," she said, not bothering to suppress her grin.

"I'm glad you find this all so amusing," Schmidt was so mad he was practically bouncing in his chair. "I personally find it hard to laugh at the misfortunes of the university I love."

"Oh, come on, Orville, stop being so stuffy. You know as well as I do that Keith was—is—a damn sight more interested in what a gift from Bach could do for his own prestige than what it might accomplish for the school."

Schmidt opened his mouth to reply, but Wolfe had had enough of the skirmish. He held up a hand to silence him. "Mrs. Moreau, I should think that after the Bach episode, Mr. Potter, too, would qualify as an antagonist of Hale Markham's."

"Without question," Elena said promptly. "For that matter, he didn't much care for Hale even before the incident. Almost from the moment Keith arrived on campus, Hale was constantly questioning his policies and his judgment. So were a lot of the rest of us, but Hale was always more outspoken about it."

"Hale was outspoken about *everything*," Greenbaum piped up. "He'd give you an argument if you said it looked like rain. Talk about opinionated." He caught Wolfe's eye and clammed up.

"Well, at least he *had* some opinions," Elena said pointedly. "Mr. Wolfe, Hale may not have been the most popular person on the Prescott campus, but he likely was the frankest."

"Frankness is a saber with two well-honed edges," Wolfe remarked, draining the beer from his glass and refilling it from the second bottle. I tucked that away, figuring it might come in handy someday. "True, it may enhance one's reputation for candor, but it frequently serves as a lodestone for resentment as well—to say nothing of stronger emotions. Do you care to add to Mr. Markham's roll of enemies?"

Elena's eyes slid from Schmidt to Greenbaum and back again. "I don't think so," she said.

"Very well. Mr. Schmidt, you've been patiently awaiting your turn, and I appreciate your forbearance. You have the floor."

Schmidt accepted a fresh bourbon on the rocks from me with a curt nod and turned back to Wolfe. "If you're trying to set me up, I'd advise you to forget it," he said. "It's common knowledge that Hale and I didn't much care for each other. He saw me, I know, as a rabid left-winger teetering on the brink of Marxism. And he resented my getting named department chairman a few years back when he figured he should have had the job."

"How did you feel about him?" Wolfe asked, lacing his fingers over the high point of his middle.

"Professionally, I thought he was an above-average classroom instructor, a fair researcher, inarguably a better-than-average writer, an erratic theoretician, and a shameless self-publicist. On a personal level, I found him arrogant, dogmatic, rude, and altogether insufferable. I formed those views years ago, and I've never had occasion to revise them."

"Did the two of you openly clash?"

"You've of course been talking to people around campus." Schmidt allowed himself the hint of a smile. "I think it's accurate to say we had our moments in departmental meetings. Although from my perspective, Hale was the instigator of most of our . . . shall we say, public differences. He was always looking to pick a fight."

"What about the satirical article he wrote soon after your book was published?"

"You *do* have your sources," he said, nodding and forcing a smile. "Well, what about it?"

"Come, come, Mr. Schmidt. Surely such an article must have exacerbated the rancor between you."

"Well, of course it did!" Schmidt barked, leaning forward with his palms on his knees. "What did you expect? It was a mean-spirited, gratuitous, and utterly uninformed pile of bilge, written for one reason: to irritate me."

"It appears to have done so."

Schmidt reddened. "I was angry, damn angry. No sense denying it. I had good reason to be, for God's sake. The man was an absolute piranha. You know, he did more than just write that piece about my book. He also sent copies of his poison anonymously to book reviewers all over the East Coast, and maybe elsewhere, too, for that matter. He knew most of them wouldn't have seen that reactionary little rag where it ran."

"How do you know Mr. Markham was the sender?" Wolfe asked.

"Hah, that one's easy. After a friend who runs the book column of a small New Jersey paper told me he'd gotten a photocopy of the piece in the mail, I confronted Hale, and the bastard just laughed in my face and said something like 'Well, isn't that curious?' It was obvious from his reaction that he was the Lucifer. My New Jersey editor friend checked around for me and found out that at least eight other newspapers received photocopies—all without a covering letter or return address. Needless to say, I didn't get reviewed a lot. As much as I hate to admit it, Hale's name on that slimy article carried a lot of weight."

"I'd have to agree," Greenbaum put in, nodding vigorously. Wolfe shot a glance his way and turned back to Schmidt, who looked like he'd rather be somewhere else. "Mr. Schmidt, I'll ask you the same question I posed to Mrs. Moreau: Can you suggest any other enemies Mr. Markham had?"

"Oh, let's get serious. What is it you're *really* asking? Did I give Hale a shove? The answer, if it's any of your business, is an emphatic, unequivocal no! For that matter, neither did anybody else, whatever Walter Cortland thinks. Why can't you accept the fact that Hale accidentally fell into the Gash? I know it's hard for you to comprehend, being from New York and all, but accidents really do happen, and you heard Elena say he'd had some fainting spells. Not every death has to be a murder, although I recognize that accidental death hardly makes good copy for newspapers or big fees for lawyers—or private investigators."

Wolfe grimly considered Schmidt, then shifted his attention to his beer. He was silent for so long that I thought he was counting the bubbles dancing their way to the top of the glass, but just as I was about to say something to break the spell, he leveled his eyes at Greenbaum. "Sir, how did you feel about Mr. Markham?"

The lanky professor twitched his bony shoulders. "What do you mean, how did I feel?"

"I thought the question was manifestly clear, but I will restate it," Wolfe said. "How did you and Mr. Markham get along?"

Greenbaum twitched again, this time the legs as well as the shoulders. He was as bad as Cortland. Must be some kind of academic affliction. "Hale was a respected colleague, one I'd known for years," he said defensively. "He brought a lot of honor to the school."

"Would you term him a friend?"

"Hardly."

"But you had been friends at one time, I believe?"

"I'm not sure I know what you're driving at."

"On the contrary, Mr. Greenbaum, I think you do. You were a disciple of Mr. Markham's years ago, a devoted follower, and then a rift occurred."

"That sounds suspiciously like the gospel according to Walter Cortland," Greenbaum said peevishly. "Well, I'm sure he spun quite a tale to you about how I deserted Hale and his philosophy and principles—it's a story he's been telling for years to anyone he can get to listen, sort of like the Ancient Mariner at the wedding feast, although I must say, it's getting pretty damned threadbare around the edges. The truth is, Hale and I both changed; it wasn't a unilateral move on my part. Over the years, Hale got more conservative—a *lot* more conservative— while I moved toward the center."

"I'd say well past the center," Elena observed with a mocking smile. Greenbaum sent her a look that told her he wasn't amused and turned back to Wolfe.

"Anyway, I was going through a long period of philosophical reevaluation," he continued. "That reevaluation admittedly included some shifts in my views— hardly an unprecedented occurrence. But Hale became furious with me for 'deserting the noble army' as he termed it. In Hale Markham's world, if you weren't with him—and with him one hundred percent—you were against him. There was no middle ground."

"Was the breach between you a sudden one?" Wolfe asked.

Greenbaum's narrow head bobbed up and down. "Very. It practically happened overnight. I was fortunate to have Orville there to supply moral support and encouragement. Hale stopped speaking to me altogether. We'd pass in the hall or on the campus, and he'd look right through me. Like I wasn't there at all."

"What was Mr. Cortland's attitude toward you at this time?"

"Walter? Oh, he was cool, at least for a while, but never arctic like Hale. That's not his nature. He's always been civil, at least. As Mr. Goodwin has now seen, we even share the same table at lunch with some frequency."

"And you and Mr. Markham never reconciled your differences?"

"No. Hale eventually deigned to talk to me again, but only when it was absolutely necessary, usually because of some matter of university business."

"And what about departmental meetings?"

"Ah, you've talked to Walter about that, too, no doubt. So he probably told you how Hale and I butted heads."

"I can speak to that," Schmidt said, leaning forward and jabbing a pudgy finger at the air. "A few of our meetings got a little . . . stormy. But as I said before, it was invariably Hale causing the storm. It seemed as if whenever Ted said something, Hale would maliciously contradict him. For that matter, he contradicted me every chance he got for a while, too. Some of those sessions were nightmares to try to chair." His face clearly indicated that the memory of these meetings wasn't pleasant.

"Even recently?" Wolfe asked.

"Oh, maybe a little less in the last year or so," Schmidt conceded. "Hale wasn't quite as antagonistic as he had been."

"Frankly, I didn't notice much mellowing on his part," Greenbaum objected, throwing a glare at Schmidt. Apparently he figured they should present a united front. "At a meeting just last spring, I think it was in May, he called me a son of a bitch—not once but twice. Surely you can't have forgotten that episode, Orville."

"I haven't, not by any means, but in fairness to Hale, I think he was being more of a curmudgeon than an antagonist when he said that. He was going out of his way to be difficult, and to get attention."

"The words have the same impact regardless of the intention," Greenbaum sniffed, his breathing coming quickly. "I know what's said about speaking ill of the dead, but the man was a barbarian. I'm going to tell you all something that only Orville here has heard, to give you an idea what kind of person we're talking about. Almost exactly one year ago, after a particularly tense departmental meeting—Orville remembers the one—in which we really went at each other, Hale caught up with me out in the hall. I'll never forget it; he stuck his face right up to mine and hissed that if he never accomplished anything else, he'd get me off the faculty. Those were his precise words: 'If I never do another thing, I'll see the day you're gone from here.'" He looked around, as if expecting one of us to gasp at the announcement. Our silence appeared to dismay him.

"What Ted says is true—he told me about it later, and he was still shaking," Schmidt said. "But I told him then that his job was as secure as a Scotsman's grip on his wallet. After all, we're talking about tenure here."

"Tenure is indeed a powerful shield," Wolfe agreed mildly. He had strong views on the subject, I know.

"Oh, I wasn't so much worried about Hale trying to mount a campaign against me." Greenbaum frowned. "What really worried me was that he'd get . . . *violent*. I honestly feared for my safety. He could be—"

"Ted, why don't you shut the hell up?" The female voice crashed like the thunder of a midsummer Ohio downpour. Elena twisted at her end of the sofa, turning toward Greenbaum like a tiger ready to leap. For an instant, I thought she was going to reach across and whack him one, but she drew a deep breath, which seemed to calm her, although the look she kept giving him told me to never go out of my way to get her mad.

Wolfe considered his glass of beer, which he apparently found to be the most interesting thing in the room. "Mr. Greenbaum, after that confrontation in the hallway, did Mr. Markham ever threaten you again?"

Greenbaum glanced nervously at Elena before opening his narrow mouth. "Uh, no, not like that. We had words a few more times in departmental meetings, but nothing like that time."

Wolfe glared, directing his expression first at Elena, then at Greenbaum, and finally at Schmidt, proving that he was an equal-opportunity glarer. "The conversation has been most instructive," he said, pulling in most of the room's oxygen before exhaling. "Before you leave, however, I would like to pose a single question to each of you: Can you account for your actions on the night that Hale Markham died?"

"By God, I knew that was coming!" Schmidt roared, pounding his fist into the palm of his other hand, which would have hurt if his hands hadn't been so chubby. "The obligatory 'where-were-you-on-the-night-of-the-murder?' that the fictional detective invariably asks. God's in his heaven—All's right with the world. Tennyson."

"Browning," Wolfe corrected. "God may indeed be in his heaven, but patently we're elsewhere. Mr. Schmidt, since my query elicited such animation from you, why don't you respond first?"

Orville Schmidt slouched in his chair and considered Wolfe from under bushy eyebrows. "I'll have to look at the appointment calendar in my office," he said. "After all, that was what, over a month ago?"

"Three weeks," Wolfe countered promptly. "September twenty-third, a Wednesday."

"I'll check it when I get to my office in the morning," Schmidt said, "if only to satisfy you."

"I don't know why I have to satisfy anybody," Greenbaum mumbled. "This man's not the law."

"True," Schmidt answered. "But there are at least two factors to be considered here, Ted: First, since I have nothing to hide, why shouldn't I tell him where I was? And second, let's face it, he has clout, particularly with the

New York newspapers. I know—I've read about him and his work in them on more than one occasion. What if he decides to go to the *Gazette* or the *Times* or one of the other papers and tell them I won't talk about where I was the night Hale died? That could make me—and the university—look bad. It's not right, I grant you, but that's the way the world works."

"Mr. Schmidt, if I may interrupt," Wolfe said. "I concur completely with your first point, but take issue with your second one. It is true that Mr. Goodwin and I have for many years enjoyed amicable relations with the press, specifically the *Gazette*. However, I do not make it a practice to run indiscriminately to the newspapers in an effort to gain leverage or tarnish reputations. Mr. Greenbaum, do you know what you were doing on the night of September twenty-third?"

"Hardly. If I can paraphrase our peerless leader in the White House, 'Do *you* remember where you were on the night of the twenty-third?'"

"I do," Wolfe said, "But then, I am at home every night, this being a notable exception." I braced for a glare, but Wolfe apparently didn't feel I was worth the effort. "Mr. Schmidt says he is going to check his calendar; will you do the same?"

Greenbaum paused for a breath. "Frankly, I don't know why I should, but . . . yes, I'll see where I was that night and let you know. I was most likely at home."

"Before you get around to asking me," Elena said, "I can tell you now that I was home alone all evening, going over the first papers I'd assigned for the fall quarter. I remember that because I stayed up unusually late grading them and had only been asleep for four or five hours when I got the call about Hale. I have no Thursday classes and had planned to sleep late that morning."

"Who called you?" Wolfe asked.

"Walter Cortland. He was so choked up that I had trouble understanding him at first. Said he'd just heard about Hale through somebody he knew on the campus security staff."

"Was anyone with you at any time that night?"

"Not a soul. I go out of my way to be alone when I'm reading or grading papers."

"What time did Mr. Cortland telephone you?"

"About eight, I think. That may not sound early, but I'm basically a night person, and as I said, I always sleep late on days when I don't have classes."

Wolfe drained the last of his second bottle of beer and licked his lips. "When we began, I promised not to prolong the proceedings unnecessarily, and I will not. I thank all of you for your time and hope to be learning from both of you gentlemen tomorrow where you were on the twenty-third of last month."

"I still don't see any reason for any of this," Green-baum grumbled as he uncrossed his long legs and got to his feet. Schmidt just shook his head, while Elena, lady that she is, smiled at Wolfe and then turned to me and flashed her pearly whites again. I rose with the three of them while Wolfe of course stayed planted in his chair, and I opened the door. I got another tantalizing smile from Elena, but both men were grim-faced as they marched out. I watched them go down the hall to the stairway and then shut the door, turning to Wolfe, who had closed his eyes, probably wishing that when he opened them, he'd be back home in his chair in the office.

"Well, counting Cortland, you've now met four members of the esteemed Prescott faculty. Based on that, would you care to comment on the current state of academe in America?"

"Pfui. With the possible exception of the woman, an unimpressive array. Archie, I will want breakfast in the room at eight tomorrow. I assume it should be ordered tonight?"

I agreed and handed him the room service menu again, strongly suggesting that he make his own call this time. The experience would be good for him.

THIRTEEN

The ringing jarred me awake, and I rolled over to stop it. "Good *morn*-ing, Mr. *Good*-win," the singsong voice on the other end of the line chirped. "It's ex-*act*-ly seven-thirty, and the *tem*-perature is *fifty*-three degrees." I thanked her—I think—and slammed the receiver, missing the cradle on the first try. I'll give the Prescott Inn its due: Not only is the food good, the mattresses are three-star too, at least the one in room two-thirty-four. From the moment my head hit the pillow around eleven-forty, I don't remember a thing until Ms. Singsong's call, which, as she pointed out, came ex-*act*-ly when I'd asked for it.

Wolfe wasn't the only one getting room service. I'd placed my own order the night before: link sausage, scrambled eggs, wheatcakes, a large orange juice, milk, coffee, and the *Times*. And I'll be damned if it all didn't come, as requested, at precisely eight o'clock, after I'd showered and shaved. These folks must have been tutored by Fritz.

I ate and read the paper at the same pace as at home. After all, there was no reason to rush—our first appointment wasn't until nine-thirty, when we would be honored by a visit from the president of the university. I had a fine view out the window of the campus across the street, which looked so good in the morning sunshine that it would have made a dandy picture for a school recruitment brochure, or whatever they use these days to sell colleges to kids coming out of high school—and of course to their checkbook-toting parents as well.

At five to nine, having finished the *Times* and everything on my plate, plus the two-cup pot of coffee, I stretched, put my suitcoat on, and walked down the hall to check on Wolfe's progress with breakfast. I rapped on his door once, twice, a third time. No answer. I called out his name, and again got nothing. I started to sweat as I reached for my key to his suite. I should mention that in the brownstone, the floor of the hall outside his bedroom is rigged so that when I turn a switch in my own room before I go to bed, it will set off an alarm if anyone comes within ten feet of his door. That may sound silly to you, but more than a few people would like to read Wolfe's obituary, and some might very well want that badly enough to break into the house and plug him or stab him as he sleeps. That was on my mind as I opened the door, and I was wishing I'd slept on the sofa in Wolfe's suite. And I was angry at myself for letting down my guard simply because we weren't in Manhattan.

The sitting room was empty, except for a room service table covered with the dishes from what apparently had been Wolfe's breakfast. I went into the bedroom, dominated by a king-sized bed that had been slept in but now was empty. Ditto the bathroom. There were no indications of violence anywhere, and that probably was a good sign, although I was thinking Wolfe could have been marched out at gunpoint, which gives you an idea of my mental state.

I went out, taking the stairs down two at a time to the lobby, where a young man with wire-rimmed glasses and sandy hair parted neatly in the center was at the front desk fiddling with some paperwork. "Did you see a large man, a very large man, pass by here?" I asked, realizing as I said it that I was out of breath.

"Yes, sir, I did, the gentleman in suite two-thirty-two—Mr. Wolfe, I believe. He went out about ten minutes ago."

"Alone?"

"I think so, but I'm not sure."

He couldn't have gotten far, at least not on his own, I thought as I pushed through the front doors and looked across the street at the campus. I shot a glance left and then right along the street, vaguely conscious that the campus was pretty lively this morning.

And then I spotted him. He was standing with his walking stick next to a big oak tree about seventy yards to my right.

"Enjoying the view?" I said as I got to within a few feet of him. "I thought maybe you'd gone over to the track to jog a few laps."

He ignored my comment. "Amazing," he said. "I have counted twenty-nine students passing by—at least I assume they are students, despite their apparel—and seventeen of them had those . . . *things* . . . screwed into their ears."

"Walkmans."

Wolfe shuddered. "Unfathomable."

"Look, it's pleasant to see you having fun conducting research on the habits of *Collegius Americanus*," I said, "but couldn't you have let me know you were going out? I'm not used to this much activity on your part. You had me worried."

Wolfe turned to me and opened his eyes wide. "Indeed? I hardly thought my walking less than a city block would be of concern to you, especially given that you saw fit, through a ruse, to uproot me and to drag me halfway up the state."

"We're nowhere near halfway up the state," I fired back. "Changing the subject, how was your breakfast?"

"Passable. Dinner was better," he grumped.

"Be of good cheer. We'll be home well before the sun has kissed the horizon. And besides, think of the war stories you'll be able to regale Fritz with from this adventure. By the way, it's now after nine. Is all the exercise getting you in shape to meet with the president of the university?"

"Confound it, yes," he said, thumping his stick on the sidewalk, which for him is an act of violent physical exertion. With that, he did an almost respectable left-face and marched back to the Prescott Inn.

Twenty minutes later we were in the suite, Wolfe settled in his semicomfortable chair and me in the same one I'd occupied the night before. We were working on a fresh pot of coffee that had just been brought up by a tall, gaunt waiter—our short-and-smiley friend apparently was off duty—when the phone rang. It was Potter, calling from the lobby to make sure we were there, and I told him to come ahead.

I stood just outside our door to greet him when he strode along the hall from the stairway, looking every bit as dapper and successful and self-confident as he had when I'd seen him at a distance in the Student Union two days earlier. "Good morning, I'm Archie Goodwin," I said cheerfully, ushering him into the room and introducing him to Wolfe, whom he eyed speculatively. "Mr. Wolfe," he said in a Ted Kennedy voice that made me wonder if he'd practiced it, "I've heard a great deal about you; it's an honor to meet you," he said without conviction, taking a seat on the sofa, accepting my offer of coffee, and unbuttoning the coat of his custom-tailored suit, this one a sleek blue three-piece job. "Although I must admit I'm somewhat puzzled by the reason for your visit. Walter was cryptic, to say the least, when he told me on the phone of your desire to meet with me. Something about Hale Markham possibly having been murdered, I believe?" He fingered the knot of his striped silk tie.

"Possibly, to use your word," Wolfe said, setting his coffee cup on the end table. "Although that is yet to be determined to my satisfaction."

"But it was ruled an accident," Potter insisted, frowning. "There was no indication of foul play, as I believe you people like to call it. Besides, who would have wanted to kill Hale, for heaven's sake?"

"That's what Mr. Goodwin and I are trying to determine, sir. We're hoping you can help us."

"I'll do what I can, of course," Potter answered, spreading his hands. "But I'm sure that if there were even the slightest chance that Hale had been murdered, the police would be investigating, and I haven't heard anything from them to indicate that this is the case."

"If you'll indulge me, please," Wolfe said. "I understand Mr. Markham had been antagonistic toward one of the school's prospective benefactors, Leander Bach?"

"Oh, that business." Potter dismissed it with a wave of the hand. "The school paper blew it all out of proportion, as papers, particularly those that are student-run, tend to do." He beamed at Wolfe paternally, which didn't go over big.

"Isn't it true, however, that Mr. Markham publicly decried Mr. Bach's bequest?"

Potter considered the question, then nodded grimly. "He said something in one of his classes, yes. But then, Hale always had been outspoken."

"And isn't it also true that because of his remarks, both in the classroom and in the campus newspaper interview, Mr. Bach withdrew his offer?"

Potter took a deep breath and then a sip of coffee, dabbing his lips deliberately with his napkin. "Leander was upset, and I can't say that I blame him. After all, here's a man who was ready to give his alma mater an unprecedented gift. An incredible gift. Word of it got out—I don't honestly know how, but universities, Mr. Wolfe, are like small towns—and that's when Hale unloaded. I still think things would have been all right if the paper hadn't picked up on what he said. When Leander found out, he was—well . . . angry, to say the least. Felt like he'd been ill-used. I think you can understand that."

"I can indeed. The benefactor spurned. Did he and Mr. Markham ever talk after that?"

"Lord, no!" Potter's handsome mug expressed horror. "I'm not sure they ever talked even *before* that. Hale had no use for Bach, and Leander obviously wanted nothing to do with Hale after what happened. In fact, he'd never much cared for Hale's, uh, politics, to say the least."

Wolfe fixed his gaze on the president. "It's been said, I believe, that after what happened, Mr. Bach would never give a cent to Prescott as long as Hale Markham remained on the faculty."

"Who said that?" Potter jerked forward, spilling a sip's-worth of coffee on his trouser leg. But he didn't seem to notice it. "I never heard it."

Wolfe raised his shoulders a fraction of an inch and then lowered them. "Perhaps it was just talk. What is Mr. Bach's attitude about a gift to the school now?"

"That's confidential," Potter said stiffly.

"Come now, Mr. Potter," Wolfe said, leaning forward in his overburdened chair. "Mr. Goodwin and I are not here to generate exclusive stories for some newspaper. We are interested in learning the circumstances of Mr. Markham's death, and I submit that our interests and yours coincide—or at least they should."

"But I'm already satisfied that his death was accidental," Potter said, running a hand lightly over his dark, well-styled hair and looking pleased with himself. "Why should I put up with your interrogation just because one of Markham's chums mistakenly thinks he was murdered? I assume Walter Cortland is your client."

Wolfe met Potter's gaze. "Why indeed should you have to put up with this—specifically, with me? As president of the university, the whole university, not just segments or special interests within it, you are naturally expected to be concerned with everything affecting the institution, how it functions, how it is perceived. If a murder has been committed—and I am not ready to state this as fact—your lack of cooperation would surely find its way to light."

"With your help?" Potter said sharply.

Wolfe shrugged again, saying nothing. Fifteen seconds passed, then thirty. I thought Potter was going to skedaddle, but when he got halfway out of the chair, he sank back again, looking suddenly very tired.

"All right," he sighed. "I'm going to take a chance and trust you. What relatively little I know about your reputation is positive." His tone became very earnest; it was a nice performance. "Mr. Wolfe, the fact is that Leander has now committed to give the university a sum, a magnificent one, I'm proud to say. But please, I beg you to keep this confidential. You saw what happened the last time this kind of news slipped out."

"And he made this commitment after Mr. Markham's death?"

"Yes."

"So Mr. Markham could truly be said to have stood in the way of this gift?"

This time it was Potter's turn to shrug. "I'd prefer not to think of it in those terms."

"How would you describe your relationship with Mr. Markham, particularly recently?"

"So this *is* an inquisition. All right, I'll tell you; I didn't like him, and he didn't like me. I found Hale Markham to be high-handed, arrogant, intransigent, and intolerant of the views of others to the point of obnoxiousness. And frankly, I don't think he made the good of the school primary. He was interested first, last, and always in what benefited Hale Markham and Hale Markham alone. Am I glad he's dead? No—of course not; he was a superb teacher and a scholar of the first order. Am I happy we're getting that contribution from Leander Bach? You're damn right I am, very happy. If that seems contradictory, so be it. . . ." Potter leaned forward and screwed up his well-tended face, as if trying to recall something. "You know, there *was* something that happened, just a few days before Hale died, I think, maybe three or four. I hadn't thought much about it, what with it being typical of him."

"Yes?" Wolfe prompted.

Potter fingered a blue Wedgwood cuff link. "Before I go on, I want you to know I don't believe this had any significance, given what happened later. Still, it was interesting. Hale came to see me one afternoon. He'd actually called the day before and asked for an appointment—if you're interested in the specific date, my secretary surely has it on her calendar. Anyway, I remember thinking at the time—hoping, really—that Hale was coming to tell me he planned to retire. That wasn't it, though. Mr. Wolfe, are you aware that Orville Schmidt has recently completed a book?"

Wolfe nodded. "The tome on George Marshall and the Truman Doctrine?"

"Correct. Well, although it isn't out yet, won't be for another month or so, Hale had somehow got hold of bound galleys or a review copy. He had just finished reading it and he came storming in to say that he spotted six places where material was blatantly plagiarized from previous books on the subject or the period. He claimed whole paragraphs were lifted, practically verbatim, without attribution and with only a word or two changed."

"Indeed? What did he intend to do with this information?"

"That's the interesting thing," Potter said, pausing for coffee. "He told me he merely wanted me to know about it. He said something like 'I stirred things up enough when Orville's other book came out; I'm sitting this one out. But you should know in case there's a flap.'"

"Did you get the impression that Mr. Markham was going to divulge his discovery to others?"

"Not really. Although knowing Hale, it wouldn't surprise me if he planned to let Orville know what he'd found, if only to watch him squirm."

"Did you verify Mr. Markham's findings?" Wolfe asked.

Another shrug. "No, although he gave me a list of the sources from which Orville allegedly lifted the material. As far as I was concerned, he—Hale, that is—was drawing an inordinate degree of satisfaction from the whole matter. I found it graceless. Now, is there anything else you'd like to know? If not, I really should be on my way. I've got a full calendar today."

"I thank you for giving me a few of your precious minutes, Mr. Potter," Wolfe said dryly. "Before you leave, can you account for your time on the night Hale Markham died—the twenty-third of last month?"

"My God, you've got crust," Potter said, spacing his words for effect in a Kennedy-esque voice just above a whisper. "I've just leveled with you, told you something highly confidential, and then *this*." The man should be on Broadway.

But the president's histrionics fell on deaf ears. "Mr. Goodwin and I have made the same request of several others. All of them either have accounted for their time on that date or promised to consult their appointment books and report to us. Does this request cause you a particular problem?"

"No—why should it?" Potter said, obviously struggling to stay unruffled. "I'll check when I get back to the office, if you want to call me. But let me say this," he puffed. "You'd better not do anything to damage this school in any way or, by God, I'll take both of you to court, and I mean it." With that, he rose, squared his shoulders pompously, walked out, and slammed the door behind him.

"Not a half-bad exit," I said. "Reminds me of the way Bogart blew his stack for effect and marched out of the D.A.'s office in *The Maltese Falcon*."

Wolfe glowered at me. He knew of course that I knew he'd never seen the movie, and it always peeves him when I make a reference to something he can't respond to. Never mind that he does that kind of thing to me all the time.

FOURTEEN

Now that Potter had been disposed of, we were down to our final session at Prescott—with Gretchen Frazier, who was due at eleven. Wolfe stayed glued to the chair that he had been parked in for the better part of the last twenty-four hours, with his book in front of his face. I contemplated asking if he wanted me to call downstairs and order beer, but thought better of it. After all, it was only ten-forty-four; if we had been at home, he'd still be up in the plant rooms, and with so many of his other routines already messed up, I didn't want to throw off his drinking schedule, too. Some things deserve to remain sacred.

It was almost quarter after eleven when the telephone squawked. "Nero Wolfe's room," I answered.

"Sorry I'm late, Mr. Wolfe," an out-of-breath Gretchen Frazier said between pants. "I'm calling from a house phone in the lobby. What room are you in?"

I told her, and less than a minute later, I was holding the door open for her. She looked younger than she had before, maybe because she was wearing a white blouse, pleated skirt, and tennis shoes. "Oh, I'm sorry I couldn't come last night," she began without recognizing me. "On Thursday nights, I teach an aerobics class to a group of— wait a minute, you're—Mr. *Goodman*, isn't it? You . . . you're the one I had coffee with. The one whose nephew is . . . what are *you* doing here? Professor Cortland asked me to see Nero Wolfe. And I—"

"Miss Frazier, may I present Nero Wolfe," I cut in,

bending at the waist and making a sweeping gesture toward him with an outstretched arm. Wolfe set his book down, sent a glare my way, and turned toward our guest, dipping his head at least an eighth of an inch. That's his all-purpose greeting, which he feels is a more-than-adequate substitute for a bow or a handshake, whether the person to whom it is directed is male or female.

She looked at me, then at Wolfe and back to me. I'd almost forgotten how blue her eyes were.

"Miss Frazier, please have a seat," Wolfe said. "Before you go on, an explanation is in order. This gentleman, whom you know to be Arnold Goodman, is Mr. Archie Goodwin, and he is in my employ. On an earlier visit to Prescott, he chose to represent himself as a Mr. Goodman. I neither defend nor decry his action, but I appreciate your confusion. Do you have any questions relating to Mr. Goodwin's masquerade?"

She looked flustered for an instant and then shrugged. "Well . . . yes, I *do* have a question," she said, nodding, "although not so much about the—what did you call it—masquerade? Professor Cortland said you wanted to see me because you think Hale—Professor Markham—was . . . killed?"

"Not technically correct," Wolfe said. "But first, can we get you anything to drink? Coffee, perhaps?"

"No, nothing, thank you." She balanced on the edge of the chair as if she were going to leap up and run out at any moment. "I'm in kind of a hurry and I'd like to be home in less than an hour. I'm behind schedule on two papers."

"We will respect the demands upon your time. As to your question, it is Mr. Cortland who thinks his colleague was murdered, and he has asked Mr. Goodwin and me to undertake an investigation."

"Murder?" she said, shaking her head and screwing up her face. "I don't believe it. No way! It's bad enough he's dead. Why would anybody want to murder him?"

"Madam," Wolfe said, still trying to find ways to get comfortable in his chair, "I'm not now prepared to state that Mr. Markham died at someone else's hand, but I concede the possibility exists. You do not?"

Gretchen shook her head again, her face showing more dismay than denial. "I . . . I don't know."

"Very well. How *do* you think Mr. Markham met his death?" Wolfe asked.

"An accidental fall, like the reports said."

"But was not Mr. Markham a mountain climber and hiker, very surefooted?"

"Ye-e-e-s, but anybody can get careless and slip. There's no other explanation."

"So it would seem," Wolfe said. "Do you know how Mr. Markham felt about Elena Moreau?"

"What?" The question surprised Gretchen, as Wolfe had intended, and she brushed her hair out of her face. "Oh, Dr. Moreau—I know they were good friends. I think they'd known each other for a long time."

"How would you describe their relationship?"

"Good friends," she repeated, with tension edging into her voice.

"I see. How would you describe the relationship between *you* and Mr. Markham?"

"In what way?" she asked, her cheeks reddening.

"Just that," Wolfe said, turning a palm over. "What was your relationship?"

"Teacher to student," she answered woodenly. "He was my adviser, and besides that, he was a wonderful professor. I admired him more than anybody else I've ever known. And I miss him terribly."

"That's understandable. Miss Frazier, where were you on the night Mr. Markham died?"

With that question, the pressure that had been building in Gretchen broke, and her tears came like one of those sudden July storms. Wolfe is uncomfortable enough around women when they're calm, but waterworks invariably send him running for cover. He was out of his chair and into the bedroom faster than when he heads for the dinner table, leaving me to comfort Gretchen Frazier for the second time in three days. I did my best, sitting next to her and handing her one of the monogrammed handkerchiefs Lily had given me on my last birthday. Her sobs continued for at least a minute before she took a couple of deep breaths.

"I'm sorry," she said, sniffling. "That wasn't very mature of me, was it? You always seem to see me crying. Please apologize to Mr. Wolfe."

"We all have to have some kind of release," I said, trying to sound sympathetic. "And I also know that you're anxious to get back to your work. But I wouldn't be doing my job if I didn't follow up on Mr. Wolfe's last question."

She nodded, still fiddling with the handkerchief. "I'm pretty sure I was at home in my apartment studying; that's where I am most evenings. Except Thursdays, you know, when I teach aerobics."

"Was anyone with you?"

"No. I live alone."

Somehow, I had expected that answer. I thanked Gretchen for her time, putting my arm on her shoulder, and I escorted her to the door, slipping on the chain lock after she had left.

"You can come out now," I said loudly to the closed bedroom door. "All's clear."

Wolfe emerged, looking grumpier than ever, and replanted himself in the chair that he had come to know and loathe.

"She's gone," I said. "After you upset her with your hard-as-nails line of questioning, I had to soothe her before I sent her on her way."

"Did you get an answer as to where she was that night?" he snarled.

"Of course. She was home and was deep into her studies—alone."

"Your opinion of her?" Wolfe was deferring to me, based on what he likes to think are my infallible instincts about women, particularly those of the species under thirty.

"Smarter than she acts—she'd have to be to make it to star-student status at the graduate level. She's somewhat on the ingenuous side, though, and I never trust that type."

Wolfe absorbed that. "Assuming that Mr. Markham's death was no accident, what odds would you place on her as the murderer?"

"You really like to put my skill in reading females to the test, don't you?" I said. "Okay, here it is: I could go six-to-five either way, but leaning slightly toward innocent. Don't ask me why—like with Elena, it's just a feeling I've got. However, I think young Gretchen knows more than she's telling. I suppose now you're going to order me to take her dancing so I can unleash my legendary charm and wrest her innermost secrets from her."

"The idea hadn't occurred to me," he said airily, raising both eyebrows.

"You know, it's quarter to twelve," I said, changing the subject. "Shall we eat here before driving back?"

Wolfe looked at me as though I'd lost my mind. "We will leave immediately. Call Fritz. Ask him what we will be having for lunch."

FIFTEEN

The drive home, I'm pleased to report, was uneventful. Not surprisingly, Wolfe alternately sulked and grimaced from his roost in the back seat, despite my rigid adherence to the speed limit, my total avoidance of tailgating, and—if I may say so—an overall superb job of driving. As we headed south in the midday sun, I commented several times on the splendor of the autumnal colors, but all I got from the rear were grunts. "Some fun you are to ride with," I snapped as we came within sight of the Manhattan skyline.

Wolfe wasn't happy until he was back inside the brownstone and at the dining room table attacking Fritz's clam cakes. Then he got positively gregarious and began to expound on why North America was so conducive to exploration and, ultimately, to settlement and development.

"Look, I don't disagree," I said between bites of a clam cake, "but I'd like to remind you that less than an hour ago, you were riding through some of the very North America you are extolling—and a most attractive part of it, I might add. I didn't hear any rhapsodizing then."

Wolfe looked at me as if he hadn't heard a word, and damned if he didn't shift gears, smoothly at that, into a discussion of why the French had never been as effective in colonization as the English—nor as enthusiastic, not only in North America but around the world. I kept on chewing.

After lunch, we had coffee in the office, where business is fair game. "Okay," I said, spinning in my desk chair to face Wolfe. "Where do we stand on Markham's death? Is it a case, or isn't it?"

"As usual you are chafing for activity, Archie, which is not in and of itself bad," Wolfe said. "You are the quintessential man of action, and I applaud your enthusiasm and energy—after all, those are the qualities that render you invaluable to me. To denigrate those qualities would be fatuous, and I will not do so."

He paused to drink, and I recognized what he was up to. He was now ready to take the case, but he wanted me to be the one to push it, so he was getting cute and trying a little flattery. Part of me got stubborn, but I also knew that if I didn't strike while he was still in a mellow mood because of his safe return home and a stomach filled with Fritz's cooking, he might lapse into his usual state—terminal laziness.

"The way I see it, Cortland is right; Markham had to have been pushed into that ravine," I said conversationally. "Fact Number One: He was an experienced hiker and climber. Fact Number Two: He knew that terrain well—he walked it every day. Fact Number Three: The ground was dry and firm at the spot where he went over the edge." I paused to look at Wolfe, whose eyes were closed. "Fact Number Four: We have heard from Elena Moreau that Markham had dizzy spells, which might explain the plunge except for one thing. The branches on the bushes at the spot where his fall began were broken so cleanly that he must have gone over the edge with some velocity—I was surprised at first that the local police hadn't wondered about it, but once I'd made their acquaintance I could see where they could overlook evidence staring them in the face. Anyway, had Markham simply stumbled or passed out and fallen like a dead-weight, those branches, at least the larger ones, would have been bent back maybe, but not snapped off like they were. There must have been a lot of momentum behind his body to cause that type of break—the kind that comes from a shove, not just a fall. And we know from Cortland that the body was carried out of the Gash by a different route, so those branches weren't broken by anybody lugging the body back up."

He drew in more coffee, finishing the cup. "We haven't heard from any of the gentlemen yet as to where they were on the night Mr. Markham died. I suggest you call them now and get their answers."

"Potter, Schmidt, and Greenbaum?"

"And Mr. Cortland as well."

"You want me to ask our client where he was that night, too?"

"I do," Wolfe said, ringing for beer and starting in on his new book, *Hold On, Mr. President*, by Sam Donaldson.

I shrugged and opened my notebook to look up Cortland's numbers. I thought about trying his office, if only to hear the dulcet tones of Ms. Auburn-Hair, but then I remembered that somewhere along the way, the professor had mentioned he didn't have either office hours or classes Friday afternoons. I dialed his home number and he answered after four rings. "It's Archie Goodwin," I said cheerfully, as Wolfe set down the book and picked up his instrument.

"Mr. Goodwin, I'm glad you called!" He sounded as if he meant it. "I was just getting ready to call *you*. The police did phone me last night. They asked if I would come down to the station."

"Did you?"

"Of course. They—actually it was the chief—Chief Hobson—wanted to know why I had hired you and Mr. Wolfe. I must say his manner wasn't very gracious."

I kept my voice somber. "What did you tell him?"

"I reminded him what I had said at the commencement of their so-called investigation—that I was convinced Hale's demise was not accidental, and that, in the face of their obstinate refusal to delve deeper into the matter, I had turned to Mr. Wolfe. That merely increased his ire, though, and he opined that it was unwise of me to go off and get some 'high-rolling New York hotshot'— and that was the exact terminology he employed—who would come up to Prescott and start stirring things up just to get publicity for himself."

I looked to see Wolfe's reaction, but his face remained impassive. "Did the chief say he'd look into Markham's death?" I asked.

"Oh, kind of." Cortland sounded disgusted. "But it was patently obvious from his manner that he really wasn't very interested and still didn't believe Hale was murdered. He seemed more intent on inveigling me into dismissing Mr. Wolfe. When I refused, he informed me that you and Mr. Wolfe had better watch out, and that if you pulled any shenanigans in his jurisdiction, he'd see that your licenses got pulled."

"Forewarned is forearmed," I said, winking at Wolfe, who scowled in return. "Have you heard from any of the people we talked to last night and this morning?" Cortland said he hadn't, and then asked how the questioning had gone. I gave him a brief rundown—after all, he *was* our client—and then got around to a question a private detective doesn't normally pose to a client: *Where were you at the time the crime took place?* Actually, my wording went like this: "Oh, by the way, Mr. Cortland—can you remember where you were on the night that Mr. Markham died?"

There was a pause on his end, then he cleared his throat noisily. "Why on earth would you pose that, uh, question to me?" he asked sharply.

"I'm merely trying to get everyone placed that night between ten and midnight," I answered matter-of-factly. "It helps Mr. Wolfe organize his thinking." I winked at Wolfe again.

"I was at home, grading midterms," Cortland sniffed.

"Alone?"

"Of course! As I'm sure I've told you, I'm a bachelor. I live alone." He sounded offended.

"Right, you did tell me. Say, by any chance do you know where I can reach those Three Musketeers—Potter, Schmidt, and Greenbaum—right now?"

Cortland still sounded put out, but after consulting his school directory, he gave me the office and home number of each. I thanked him and signed off, promising he'd be hearing from Wolfe or me again soon. He didn't sound impressed.

"I do believe we've gone and gotten our client miffed," I told Wolfe. "That's the chance he takes, though, when he hires a high-rolling New York hotshot like you."

"Archie, your humor wears thin. You have more calls to make." With that bit of harrumphing out of the way, he rang for beer and picked up his book again. Some people simply can't take a joke.

For no particular reason, I called Schmidt first, trying his office number. A female with a voice not nearly as pleasant as Ms. Kearns's informed me none too politely that Mr. Schmidt was never in his office on Friday afternoons. I thanked her anyway, figuring she'd had a rough week.

I dialed Schmidt's home number and scored. "Hi, this is Archie Goodwin," I said, "calling to find out if you'd had a chance to check your calendar for September twenty-third."

"Oh, it's Arnold-Archie, is it?" he said with a brittle chuckle. "Yes, I looked at it first thing when I got to the office this morning. I had no meetings or other activities that night, so I must have been at home."

"Was someone with you?"

"Alas, no, I'm afraid I'm totally without alibi," Schmidt answered in a tone of mock seriousness, followed by another chuckle. "My wife was in California the last two weeks of September visiting her mother, so I was all alone. Does that vault me straight to the top of your fabled list of suspects?" I ignored the remark and thanked Schmidt for his time. My mother taught me to always be polite to everyone, even jerks.

Next I called Greenbaum at his office, and wouldn't you know it, I got the same woman, who gave the same answer in the same tone that she had three minutes earlier; I would have thanked her again if she hadn't hung up on me. I then tried Greenbaum at home; no answer. During my last few calls, Wolfe had remained hidden behind his book, but as I learned long ago, that didn't mean he wasn't paying attention. As I started to dial Keith Potter's office number, he set the book down and leaned forward.

"I assume you're going to try Mr. Potter next?" he asked.

"Oh, I thought I might. Why?"

Wolfe's reply was to dip his head slightly, which passes for a nod. It also was his way of indicating that he'd be listening in, too. Surprisingly, Potter answered himself, which forced me to adjust my opinion of him upward at least slightly. However, his reaction when he found out who was calling made me cancel the adjustment.

"My God," the president said, "I really didn't think you'd have the gall to persist."

"Just following orders," I said.

There was a silence of several seconds. "All right," he snapped, "hold on while I check my book." Another silence, this one lasting a half-minute. When he came back on the line, he sounded pleased with himself. "Let's see . . . on the twenty-third, I had a breakfast with the chairman of the English Department . . . a ten-o'clock meeting with the provost to go over the schedule of activities for Homecoming . . . lunch at the Union Building with several members of Prescott's New York City Alumni Club. At three P.M., I was interviewed—for well over an hour, at that—by a reporter from *University Management* magazine who is doing a series of profiles of presidents of major schools. I went home about five, as I remember, to change for a banquet at the same place you stayed, the Prescott Inn. Cocktails were at seven, dinner at eight. It kicked off a campaign to raise funds for a new field house. The one we have was built more than forty years ago and holds only four thousand for basketball games."

"Truly a pity," I said. "What time was the dinner over?"

"Oh . . . probably ten-fifteen, something like that. I went straight home from there."

"You drove?"

"Mr. Goodwin, Prescott, unlike New York, is a

genuinely safe place, day or at night, despite your employer's attempts to turn a tragic accident into a murder. I *walked* home. My house is only four blocks from the Prescott Inn."

"Were you alone?"

A deep breath. "Yes, I was alone. And I recall that my wife was still up reading when I got home. Can we end this interrogation now, Mr. Goodwin? I think I've been generous enough with my time and patience."

I was about to thank him when Wolfe signaled me. "Mr. Wolfe would like to say something to you," I said. "Hold the line."

Before Potter could protest, Wolfe was talking. "I appreciate your time and patience, but I am going to presume further on your good nature. I would like to meet Leander Bach."

"Then I suggest you call him for an appointment," Potter said sharply. "His office is in Manhattan, as you probably know."

"I am aware of that, but I am hoping you will intercede for me."

"Why on earth should I?"

"As I said when we talked yesterday, in the matter of Mr. Markham's death, our interests—the university's and mine—should coincide. We both seek the truth."

"I don't see how Leander could possibly be of any help to you. Despite the animosity he and Hale Markham felt toward each other, I'm not even sure they ever met."

"You're very likely correct on both counts," Wolfe conceded. "Nevertheless, I feel a conversation with him could prove to be helpful."

Another deep breath on Potter's end. "All right, I'll call him and tell him you want to see him. But I assure you I won't prejudice him in your favor. I still don't approve of what you're doing."

"Your candor is admirable, sir," Wolfe said. "Will you phone him today?"

"Yes, right now! Good-bye!" Potter banged down his receiver.

"Pretty rude for a university president," I observed,

hanging up, too, and swiveling to face Wolfe. "I don't think I'll bequeath any of the Goodwin family fortune to that field house. What do you think seeing the tycoon will accomplish?"

"Perhaps nothing," he said, lifting his shoulders slightly and then dropping them. "But at least Mr. Bach will be prepared for our call. And if he's as curious by nature as I suspect, he'll want to know what we are up to."

"So a call to Bach is the next order of business?"

"One of them. You said that when the Prescott police interrupted you in Mr. Markham's house earlier this week, you had been there only a few minutes. Am I correct that you feel a need to return?"

"It's been on my mind," I admitted. "I was going to suggest it this morning, but I wanted to get you back here as quickly as possible. I'll go tomorrow."

"I appreciate your solicitude," Wolfe said. "And I also appreciate that this will make a third trip to that place for you in a single week." The very thought drove him to pour the second bottle of beer into his empty glass.

"All in the line of duty. After all, as you yourself said a few minutes ago, I am the quintessential man of action, remember? This time, though, I'm going to take Cortland with me to Markham's house, as a buffer against that group of lads who comprise Prescott's finest."

Wolfe reached for his book. "I was going to suggest that myself, of course," he said.

Of course.

SIXTEEN

Saturday morning at quarter past eight, I once again was piloting the Mercedes north up the Henry Hudson Parkway. As much as I enjoy being behind the wheel, this was starting to get tiresome, but I wasn't about to complain; after all, the project had been my idea, and Wolfe *was* at work, or at least giving orders.

After Wolfe's "suggestion" that I might want to run up to Prescott and finish going through Markham's house, I called Cortland and got a cool reception. He was still in a sulk about being treated like a suspect, but he softened when I told him what I wanted to do.

"By all means, you should come and see the house again. This time, we can take my car. The police recognize it, and if they happen to drive by, they're not likely to stop."

I told him that sounded good and that I'd be at his place no later than ten. I also kept calling Greenbaum at home, and finally got him on the fifth try. If Cortland's initial reaction to me had been chilly, Greenbaum's was positively glacial, and he never did thaw out. He said his calendar had no evening notation for September twenty-third and that he probably spent it at home with his wife.

"Would you have left at any time?" I asked.

"Mr. Goodwin, I leave the house every night," he said, pronouncing each word deliberately. "I have a dog. His name is Alonzo, and he is a Collie. I invariably take him for a walk, and we're never gone for less than half an hour, usually from about ten-thirty to eleven. The exercise is good for both of us. We walk all over the campus and, yes, sometimes we go through the Old Oaks—I even passed Hale on his walk once about six or eight months ago when I was with Alonzo and we said hello to each other. Did I see Hale on the night he fell into the Gash? No. Did I see anything suspicious that night? No. How do I know that? Because I surely would have remembered it the next day when I heard what happened to Hale. Now I have posed the questions you were going to ask me and I have answered them. Good evening, Mr. Goodwin." He slammed down his receiver harder than he had to, but then maybe receiver banging is good therapy—everyone seemed to be doing it.

The other noteworthy event of Friday afternoon involved Leander Bach. Wolfe waited until just before his four o'clock session with the orchids to call, presumably giving Potter a chance to prepare Bach for the experience. I dialed the number of his office in the Pan Am Building while Wolfe picked up his receiver. Getting through the main switchboard to the executive suite was easy enough, and when a crisp female voice answered "Mr. Bach's office," Wolfe took over. "This is Nero Wolfe. I would like to speak to Mr. Bach. I believe Mr. Potter of Prescott University told him I would be calling."

"May I ask what this is about?" she responded.

Wolfe frowned. "I am investigating the death of Mr. Hale Markham."

"Hold the line please," she said, somewhat less crisply than before.

"Yes, may I help you? I am Mr. Bach's executive assistant." It was another female voice, this one also crisp, but with a slight southern tinge. Wolfe took a deep breath and repeated what he had told the first line of defense. "Please hold for a moment," she said.

The moment turned out to be thirty-five seconds. At this rate, Wolfe would be late for his elevator ride to the roof and Theodore would be working on an ulcer wondering what calamity could possibly cause a rupture in the precious schedule. Just when it looked like Wolfe was going to hang up and stomp out of the office, another voice came on the line.

"This is Bach. Mr. Wolfe?"

"Yes, sir. I had asked Mr. Potter to inform you I would be calling."

"Haven't heard from Keith today," the hoarse voice responded. "No matter. I know who you are, of course. What the hell, everybody does. Through the years I've read about you Lord knows how many times. What's this about an investigation into that buzzard Markham's death? What's to investigate?"

"There is reason to believe Mr. Markham's fall was not accidental."

"Eh? Well, I can guess there's a truckload of people who've considered wringing Markham's neck, but I hardly think they'd carry out the real thing. What do you want from me? I never even met the man, and I can't say I'm sorry I didn't."

"I would like to talk to you about Mr. Markham," Wolfe said. "I think your perspective would be helpful."

"Even though I never met him? Oh, hell, all right, I'll go along with this, if only to meet you. Can you come to my office Monday morning? I don't much like talking on the phone. I'm a face-to-face guy."

"I share your distaste for the telephone, sir. I make it a practice not to leave my home, however. Would it be possible for you to come here?"

"The reclusive genius bit, eh? I guess I've read about that, too. Hell, yes, I'll come—why not? But I have a practice that you should be aware of, too, and it's hard-and-fast: I never go anywhere to a meeting without my personal assistant, Miss Carswell. She was the one you spoke to before I came on the line. If I come to see you, she comes as well."

"I have no objections, sir. Let us agree on a time."

The upshot was that Bach and the indispensable Miss Carswell would come to the brownstone Sunday night at nine. That, coupled with the Saturday swing up to Prescott, effectively canceled my plans to spend the weekend with Lily at her hideaway in Dutchess County.

But she's used to cancellations from me, and she's done some canceling herself through the years. Our relationship is the kind that calls for understanding and flexibility, and we both have lots of that, at least where the other is concerned. "I'll try to enjoy myself up there alone," she had told me on the phone Friday when I called to bow out. "Just remember, I may not invite you to the country again until . . . oh, say, next weekend."

"I humbly accept and hereby vow to annihilate my eccentric and irascible employer if he dares to find chores for me that will conflict," I said, sealing our date.

I was thinking about Lily and her luxurious retreat overlooking the Hudson when the town of Prescott snuck up on me. I cruised along the picture-postcard streets, following the directions Cortland had given to his residence, which turned out to be a small white frame bungalow with green shutters just a block off the main stem and not far from the police station where I had so recently been a jewel on the cushion of Prescott police hospitality. I parked at the curb and bounded up the creaking steps to his door, giving the bell a punch.

"Ah, you're right on time, as I fully expected you would be," he said with one of his thin smiles, squinting at the sunlight as he leaned out the front door. "I suggested taking my car when you called, but it's only three blocks and the weather's nice—you may want to walk it instead."

I said I needed the exercise, so while I locked the Mercedes, Cortland went back inside for a book, then we were off down the shady streets of a town I was beginning to feel I knew. The stubby professor, this time in a corduroy sportcoat, puffed to keep up with me, and less than ten minutes later, we were on Markham's block of Clinton, which was as quiet as the other time I'd been there. "Hale loved this house," Cortland told me as we went up the front walk. "Said it was a haven for him from what he called the maelstrom of academe. I thought that after Lois died, he'd probably want to move out and take a smaller place, maybe an apartment, but he seemed perfectly content to stay here."

"Did he ever entertain?" I asked as Cortland unlocked the door.

"Almost never. Oh, maybe once every two years or so he'd have a group of graduate students over in the spring for an end-of-the-term party—beer and hamburgers, that sort of thing. Nothing elaborate, mind you. But overall, Hale wasn't much for socializing."

"Except for Elena Moreau and Gretchen Frazier?"

Cortland's ears turned red. "He used to escort Elena to various functions, yes, but as I told you before, he was five decades older than the Frazier girl," he said reprovingly. "And besides, Hale would never have permitted himself to become entangled with a student."

"It's happened before. And after all, she *is* an attractive young scholar."

Cortland looked at me as if I were depraved, something Lily has been convinced of for years. "We're here," he said, pointedly changing the subject. "Start wherever you want to and take as long as you want. If you don't mind, I'll just sit in the living room and read. If I get in your way, feel free to ask me to move."

"Fair enough. Who has been in here since Markham died?"

"Only me, and the cleaning woman. She used to work twice a week, Tuesdays and Thursdays I think, when Hale was alive, but now, I've asked her to come only every other week to dust and such."

"No realtors?"

"No." Cortland shook his head. "Although since they've learned I'm executor, several have called me endeavoring to obtain the listing. I've temporized, though, by saying any decision on selling the place will have to wait until Christina, his niece, comes to town."

"Has anything been moved out?"

"No, I haven't touched a thing, other than the article I mentioned to you, the one he'd written for that magazine, which wanted to go ahead and publish it posthumously."

"So you said. Okay, I'm going to start in his office area—that's where I was when the police came."

Cortland told me to be his guest, and he slouched in one of the easy chairs in the living room with his book while I went out to the sun porch–turned–office. It looked just the same as when I'd been so rudely interrupted by Nevins and Amundsen day before yesterday.

I sat in the comfortable, high-backed swivel chair and had a look at Markham's terminal. It was set up to take two floppy disks, but both disk drives were empty, so I didn't even bother turning the thing on. On the table, though, there was a holder with some three dozen disks in it. I pulled a batch out and shuffled through them; they were labeled everything from NOTES ON BURKE BOOK to CHECKING ACCOUNT to ELECTRIC BILLS to HOUSEHOLD EXPENSES. "Did Markham keep his whole life on the computer?" I said, turning in the direction of the living room.

"He most certainly did," Cortland answered, getting up and coming over to stand in the doorway. "Four years ago, he didn't even own a computer, but he started experimenting with one in the offices over at school one day, and he became addicted. Hale was extremely meticulous in everything he undertook, and the computer permitted him to be even more so. He was obsessive about his record keeping."

"Maybe not such a bad thing," I said. "If you don't have any objection, I'd like to take the whole batch of disks home and run them through my machine. I'll bring everything back intact."

"No objection at all, but I really doubt you'll find anything worthwhile. Please be particularly careful with the disk with the book notes on it. Hale was in the early stages of researching a new biography of Edmund Burke, and I'm optimistic I can be successful in persuading the publisher to allow me to complete it."

I told him to have no fear and started in on the rest of the house while he went back to his reading. There may be somebody in the world better at combing a place than I am, but I have yet to meet that somebody, although I admit that Saul Panzer comes close. The whole operation took me more than three hours, including the bookcases, of which there were sets in the living room, the office, and the master bedroom upstairs. I went through dresser drawers, nightstands, photo albums, stacks of old bills, file drawers of correspondence—all of it professional—storage boxes of clothes, and a basement that was cleaner than most kitchens. And nowhere did I find anything remotely helpful. Cortland popped in on me every so often to monitor my progress, but otherwise kept busy with his book, which was as fat as a dictionary and looked to be about as juicy. "I'll say this for Markham," I told him as we were getting ready to leave, "he was one well-ordered guy, or else he had the world's best cleaning woman."

"Some of both, I suppose," was his answer. "As I said earlier, Hale was extremely fastidious about his record keeping, and that sense of order and neatness carried over into everything he did. He was the antithesis of the absentminded professor stereotype, as you've obviously gathered." He grimaced. "Indeed, he often scoffed at me for my own untidiness. Have you made any significant discoveries?"

"No, and I seriously doubt there's anything in here, either," I said, gesturing to the box of disks I was carrying, "but I can't afford to ignore them, and as long as they work in our PC, I can avoid tying up any more of your time. What about Markham's office at the school?"

"We can run over there if you like, but I've pretty well gone through it, and there wasn't much to begin with—mostly papers, the majority of which Hale had already graded. He kept most of his files at home."

I told him I'd like to take a look anyway, so we walked back to his house and got the Mercedes. Markham's office was just down the corridor from Cortland's in Richardson Hall. The place was small, but infinitely neater than either Cortland's or Elena Moreau's. Markham's name was still on the door, but there wasn't much else to indicate who the tenant had been.

Twenty minutes later, I'd gone through the desk drawers and bookshelves, and I felt as frustrated as I had at his house. Walking out of the building, I asked Cortland if anybody else had helped clean out Markham's office.

"No, just me, at least as far as I know. Because I was his closest friend, as well as executor, Orville had the good sense to suggest I be the one to sift through Hale's things here. In fact, I plan to move out what little you saw there by next week, so the space can be utilized by somebody else. Space is always at a premium here on campus. Frankly, it's a depressing chore, but I guess I'd resent anybody else doing it."

I sympathized with Cortland—after all, he was talking about the man who had been, as he said, his closest friend, not to mention his mentor. I dropped him off back at his house and told him that Leander Bach was going to visit Wolfe on Sunday, and ended by giving him the stock line that he'd be hearing from us shortly. The fact that we'd be talking to Bach made him brighten slightly, but I sensed that the little guy was beginning to have doubts about having hired us.

As I headed out of Prescott for the third time in four days, I thought fleetingly about crossing the Hudson and aiming the Mercedes north toward a certain oasis on the Dutchess County side of the river. But I vetoed the idea of making a surprise appearance. I'd probably end up thinking about the case while I was there, and Lily's the kind who thrives on undivided attention. For that matter, I'm the kind who likes to give it to her.

SEVENTEEN

I got back to the brownstone at just after four, which of course meant the office was empty because the owner of the establishment was up communing with his orchids. Out in the kitchen, Fritz was doing some communing of his own, with the shrimp that would be tonight's entrée. I gave him a nod and took a carton of milk from the refrigerator; I needed something cool and soothing after the drive.

"I saved some of the marrow dumplings from lunch," he said, turning from his work. He knows I devour them by the plateful.

"Well, even though I stopped for a ham sandwich, and even though it's only three hours till dinner . . . why not?" I said with a grin, as much to please Fritz as to make my stomach happy. Two things in particular cause Fritz Brenner to fret: One, long dry spells when Wolfe isn't working, because that means money isn't flowing in to pay the mountain of expenses it takes to keep the brownstone running; and two, my eating habits when I'm away from home. And right now, Fritz was in a double-fret. I put half of it to rest by attacking the dumplings he'd saved and kept heated, declaring them as good as any he'd ever made. The other half I dealt with by telling him we were well on our way to solving the murder of Hale Markham.

Okay, so I was playing games with the truth, but what harm did it do? It sent Fritz happily back to the shrimp, and after all, there was a reasonable likelihood Wolfe would push the right buttons soon, wasn't there? At least that's what I told myself as I worked my way through the plate of dumplings.

Back in the office, fuller and more mellow, I parked in front of the computer, which sits on a small table next to my desk, and started feeding it Markham's floppy disks, figuring I'd at least have something to report to Wolfe when he came down from the plant rooms at six. I put one, labeled SENIOR SEMINAR LECTURES 1, into the PC and scrolled quickly, wondering as I read how Markham could possibly make some of this stuff interesting to his students. I went through every one of the lecture disks, and then moved on to the excitement of his monthly budgets, utilities bills, notes on various articles that would never be written, and securities portfolios and checking and savings accounts, which showed him to be comfortably set, if not exactly in the Rockefeller category. I'd gone through probably half of the stack when I heard the whirring of the elevator and, surprised, looked at my watch, which told me it was almost ninety seconds past six.

Wolfe trooped in and gave me a questioning look as he lowered his bulk into the desk chair and rang for beer. "In answer to your familiar 'what-the-hell-are-you-doing?' expression, I've been having a riveting time here at the computer," I told him. "What would you like to know about Hale Markham? I can tell you that he bought three suits in the last year, two at Reed and Struthers right here on Fifth Avenue and one at the Pickwick Shop in Prescott, and that they cost a combined total of seven hundred seventy-four dollars and change. He also bought six ties at Reed and Struthers which totaled just over ninety-two dollars. His electric bills for the first eight months of the year were—"

"Archie!" It wasn't a bellow, but it had some force.

"Yes, sir?"

"I realize this monologue is a form of therapy for you, but I am not a therapist. Report."

With that, I gave him the day's activities in Prescott, which of course weren't much. Wolfe listened and drank beer, eyeing his book several times during my narrative. When I finished, he frowned and leaned back in his one-of-a-kind chair. "What did you say to Mr. Cortland when you left him today?"

"The usual," I answered. "That we'd be back to him, and that we would be meeting with Bach tomorrow. It took all my willpower to keep from telling him you were about to crack this thing wide open and name a murderer at a televised press conference tomorrow in the Javits Convention Center. Did I do right?" That was for the therapy crack.

Not surprisingly, I got another frown. "Pfui. It appears that you have a lot more disks to go through," Wolfe observed, opening his book. I decided to let him have the last word and went back to the computerized version of "This Is Your Life, Hale Markham." I scrolled through the last year's register of personal checks; a five-year financial reporting of his speeches, for which he charged a minimum $2,500; and the text of what apparently was his standard speech, titled "Daring to Draw the Line Against the Left."

"You know," I said, turning to face Wolfe, "Markham's really made it easy for a biographer. He's got so damn much detail about himself here—there's even a disk listing the volumes he's checked out of the library." All I got from behind the book was a grunt, so I went back to discovering such things as how much the great conservative philosopher spent on new underwear and socks in a twelvemonth.

That grunt was the only noise I got out of Wolfe on the Markham affair for the next twenty-seven hours. Business is out as a subject of conversation during meals, of course, but even after dinner Saturday, he refused to talk to me about anything remotely connected with the case, hiding instead behind his book and later wrestling with a *London Times* crossword puzzle. Sunday was more of the same, with himself steadfastly ignoring my attempts to bring up what I had thought was a job we had undertaken. By midafternoon I gave up and went to a movie, leaving the lord of the manor to his book, the Sunday papers, another crossword puzzle, and some puttering in the kitchen, Fritz having taken the day off.

I got back to the brownstone at five-forty after stopping for a slice of peach pie and a glass of milk on the way home from the movie, one of those avenging-veteran-returns-to-Southeast-Asia shoot-'em-ups that was worth about a third of the admission price. But at least it took my mind off the problem at hand for a couple of hours.

I strolled into the office to find that Wolfe was having no trouble at all keeping his mind off the problem at hand. He was sitting at his desk chuckling—that's right, *chuckling*—at something he was reading in the *New York Times Magazine*, which turned out to be Russell Baker's column. "I can't tell you how pleased I am to see that you're having a good time," I said as I slid into my desk chair. "I assume you haven't forgotten that the plutocratic Mr. Bach will be stopping by later."

"I have not forgotten," he answered without looking up. I still wasn't getting anywhere drawing him into conversation, so I turned my attention to the computer, trying to decide whether to have at the last few Markham disks. After about a half-minute of debating with myself, I figured I might just as well get it over with, so I plunged ahead on the one marked LAST WILL AND TESTAMENT, which I had purposely been saving, just so I had something to look forward to. It was identical to the copy Cortland had sent us in the mail: The majority of the estate, including the house, went to his niece, with ten grand earmarked for Cortland and thousands more doled out to several politically conservative organizations. I had half expected to see Elena Moreau's name some-where along the way, but other than Cortland, there was no mention of anyone or any organization at Prescott U. I considered interrupting Wolfe with this piece of informa-tion but checked myself; I was tired of trying to get him to take his brain out of neutral, or maybe it was reverse that he was stuck in.

I went back to the remaining disks, from which I

learned that the professor was one tough grader. Of the fifty-seven students he had at the time of his death, both at the undergraduate and graduate levels, only three were in the A range as of September twenty-first, the last date marks were entered in the computer. I wasn't surprised to learn that one of those A's belonged to Gretchen Frazier. That, too, was a fact I decided Wolfe would have to do without for now.

The weekday routine in the brownstone doesn't apply on Sundays, with meals pretty much catch-as-catch-can. I knew Wolfe would be improvising in the kitchen whenever his stomach started snarling at him, and I was in no mood to eat in his company, let alone share one of his experimental concoctions, so I marched out and constructed a cucumber-and-shrimp sandwich for myself while he was still rooted to his office chair. I ate the sandwich at the small table where I have breakfast and chased it with a glass of milk, then went up to my room to rest and meditate.

Lying on my back on the bed, I went over where we were: Hale Markham found dead of a broken neck at the bottom of Caldwell's Gash, almost surely pushed. A fistful of people probably not sorry he was dead—among them the president of the university, whose principal donor had been driven away by Markham's verbal assaults; the donor, a multimillionaire industrialist, who had been held up to ridicule by Markham; the chairman of his department, whom Markham had professionally humiliated; and a fellow professor and former friend, who claimed to be afraid Markham would do him some form of bodily harm.

And then there were two attractive women, one young, one not-so-young, each of whom obviously had more than a passing interest in the virile old professor. And he obviously had had more than a passing interest in both of them as well, a situation not normally conducive to peaceful relations, academic or otherwise.

I must have turned things over in my mind several times, but I wasn't getting anywhere, and at some point I dozed off, because the next time I looked at my watch it was eight-twenty. I jumped up, went to the bathroom to splash cold water on my face and brush my hair, then put on a fresh blue shirt, maroon tie, and my gray herringbone sportcoat, the one Lily once said makes me look almost professorial.

Down in the office, I of course found Wolfe behind his desk. By now he had polished off the Sunday papers, and likely a meal of his own devising, and was wading into a new book, *The Closing of the American Mind*, by Allan Bloom. "I assume we'll offer liquid refreshments to our guests?" I asked.

He looked up and dipped his head an eighth of an inch, then went back to his reading.

"My, we're in a chatty mood. You must be saving up all your *bons mots* for our esteemed visitor."

"Archie, if you must use non-English phrases, pronounce them correctly. The 't' and the 's' in the second word are silent."

"Thanks, I needed that to keep me humble."

Wolfe set his book on the desk and looked up with raised eyebrows. "I sincerely doubt that you and humility will ever have so much as a nodding acquaintance." With that, he heaved himself upright and marched out, undoubtedly in a quest for beer. Life gets complicated for him when Fritz isn't around. I took the opportunity to set up a bar on the table in the corner, stocking it with Scotch, gin, bourbon, and mixes, as well as carafes of red and white wine that I got from the kitchen.

Wolfe had returned from his beer run and was settled back into his chair when the doorbell rang. It was nine-oh-one by my watch, which is always right. "He's not only rich, he's prompt," I said as I went out to the front hall.

I peered through the one-way glass in our front door and allowed as to how the man on the stoop looked pretty much like the Leander Bach whose picture I'd been seeing in newspapers for years: the well-tended mane of snow-white hair, the angular, ruddy face with piercing eyes, a shade of blue that even Jack Benny would have envied, and the strong chin. He was standing as straight as a cadet, and I had to admit that he looked good for a guy on the threshold of eighty.

His personal assistant looked good herself. Miss Carswell, first name as yet unknown, had honey-colored hair and a nicely arranged set of facial features that included eyes as green as her employer's were blue. If I had a Miss Carswell, I'd probably take her everywhere with me, too.

"Mr. Bach, Miss Carswell, please come in," I said, using my best let's-be-friends smile as I swung the door open. "I'm Archie Goodwin, Mr. Wolfe's assistant."

"Sir," Bach said with a businesslike nod, giving me a firm handshake. "Annette Carswell, nice to meet you," his companion said with a slight smile and a strong grip of her own. I helped her off with her coat and turned to Bach, but he already had his dark camel's hair topcoat off and onto one of the hooks in the hall. I gestured them toward the office, where I made the introductions.

Wolfe nodded, first to Bach and then to Annette—in my mind, she and I were already on a first-name basis— in such a way that they realized handshakes were to be dispensed with. I steered him to the red leather chair and her to one of the yellow chairs, giving me an opportunity to study her profile.

"I appreciate your indulging me by accepting my invitation," Wolfe said, taking them both in with the statement. "Will you have something to drink? As you see, I'm having beer."

"Thanks," the tycoon said hoarsely. "Scotch with a couple splashes of water, no ice. Time was when I'd never let water screw up a fine whiskey, but age has made me change my drinking habits—as well as a lot of other habits, for that matter. Hell, I shouldn't even have a watered-down drink, but I will." I looked at Annette, and she mouthed the words "white wine," so I hied myself over to the table to fill their orders, plus two fingers of Scotch on the rocks for myself, to be sociable.

"I didn't mind coming at all," Bach was saying as I

served the drinks. "I'm glad for the chance to meet you. You've got one hell of a reputation."

"As do you, sir," Wolfe said, dipping his head.

Bach laughed, slapping the knee of his custom-tailored gray pinstripe. "Shoot, here we are being polite when we both know damn well that we've each learned as much as possible about the other bozo. Like a good poker player, I always like to size up the people I'm sitting down with, and I suspect you do too."

"I cannot relate directly to your analogy—Mr. Goodwin is the poker player in this household—but I won't deny that I know a good deal about you," Wolfe said. "Much of it I've simply absorbed through the years from newspapers, magazines, and books—including your autobiography."

"Ah, you read *Maverick Mogul*, did you? What did you think of it? Be honest now."

"I am always honest, unless of course necessity dictates otherwise. I found the philosophy intriguing, if flawed; the narrative of your life and career interesting and sometimes compelling; the writing appallingly pedestrian."

"Hah!" Bach roared, slapping his knee again and grinning. "I like a man who speaks his piece and speaks it straight. For the record, I didn't write the damn thing myself. I hired one of those cursed ghostwriters, and I regretted it almost from the go. It served me right for being lazy. I could have written it better myself. And saved several thousand smackers in the bargain."

"I should hope so," Wolfe remarked.

"As for what I know about *you*, sir," Bach said, unfazed, "I confess I did some boning up for tonight. I've learned through sources, it doesn't matter where, that you are one smart cookie, well-read, arrogant, tough, liberal in your politics, and that the rates you charge would make an Abu Dhabi oil sheik howl, but that your clients almost always pay up without squawking."

I had all I could do to keep from laughing. First it was Cortland and his vocabulary, and now Bach and his candor. Wolfe never had had it laid out for him quite this way, and in his own office, no less. I almost felt like I should be paying admission.

One corner of Wolfe's mouth twitched slightly. "I must demur on the liberal designation," he said. "While it is true that I have espoused certain causes and principles that have come to be known popularly, if not always accurately, as 'liberal,' I wear no label, and never will."

"Well said," Bach answered promptly, taking a sip of his drink and nodding. "I don't wear any labels myself, although it's hardly a secret that I'm, shall we say, to the left of the yellow line. But to read some of the newspaper columnists, you'd think I was a member of the politburo. I know damn well it's partly because of all the trips I've made to the U.S.S.R., and the fact that I've learned to get along with a lot of those people. Hell, I *like* a lot of them. And I'm proud to do business with them. And I think doing business with them is part of the bridge building that will lead to peace. The right-wingers can't stand that kind of talk, though."

"Including Hale Markham?"

"Very good, Mr. Wolfe, very good," Bach said with an engaging grin. "You're getting back to the reason we're together, as well you should. I'm afraid it's easy for me to get off on what Annette calls tangents, at least that's what she always tells me," he said, turning to his assistant, who allowed herself a faint smile. "You said on the phone that there was reason to believe Markham's death wasn't an accident—oh, by the way, Keith Potter *did* call me, just after you did. He was hot, called you a 'loose cannon.' Said he couldn't understand why you thought Markham was shoved over that cliff. Tell you the truth, I have to take his side on that one."

Wolfe drained the beer in his glass and opened the second bottle. "There are a number of reasons for my suspicions, but I'm not yet prepared to share them. I will say, however, that Mr. Markham did not seem to be lacking enemies, or at least detractors."

"Ah, I get your drift, of course—I'm supposed to be one of those enemies. Well, to repeat something I already said on the phone, I'd never even met the man. But most of what I knew about him, I didn't like."

"For instance?"

Bach snorted. "I think you know, but of course you want to hear me say it. First off, his philosophies on government were kindergarten stuff. The guy only saw things in blacks and whites—no shadings. Second, dammit, he was a symbol of Prescott, which for my money gave the school a bad odor. Third, from all I've ever heard, he was a mean cuss to boot. Hell, I know folks have called me mean, too, but if anybody ever says I'm not fair, they've got a fight on their hands. Now Markham, he was mean *and* narrow-minded."

"But there are a great many impassioned opinions and fiercely defended convictions in the world of higher learning," Wolfe said. "It would appear that the significant point of contention between you was in the area of philosophy."

"True enough." Bach nodded. "I can't argue that."

"I understand there was trouble over a gift you had contemplated making to the university."

"That's understating it. I assume you've already delved into this, being a thorough detective, but let me give you my perspective. Through the years, I've supported Prescott financially—not with huge amounts, mind you, but steadily. I was a student there ages ago, for only a year, but it was the only college I ever had, and the place did me a hell of a lot of good, gave me some values that I like to believe I still hold. Anyway, for some time I'd been thinking about a large contribution to the school, really large. A year or so after Keith Potter became president, he and I started talking seriously about major projects, and I told him I wanted to pop for something big, felt I owed it to the place. Anyway, we met off and on for months—hell, it was more than that, it was over a year, discussing all kinds of projects. Finally I said I was prepared to give enough to build a new science building, as well as put up the seed money for a major capital campaign aimed at remodeling a whole slew of other campus buildings that had been allowed to get run-down—God knows there were plenty of them. Then—"

Wolfe held up a palm. "Mr. Bach, before you continue, a question. Is it true that you stipulated you would withhold this money as long as Hale Markham was still on the faculty?"

"Hellfire, I wish I could have made such a stipulation," Bach chuckled. "What with tenure, though, he could pretty much stay as long as he liked. When I complained about what Markham was doing to the school's image, Keith Potter did tell me that he probably wouldn't be around much longer."

"What did you take that to mean?"

"I get your drift! Not that Keith was going to shove him over that cliff, if that's where you're headed. No, I took it to mean that Keith would find a way to, shall we say . . . *encourage* his retirement."

"Were you willing to go ahead and make your gift while Markham was still actively teaching?"

"Reluctantly, because in any case, the guy wasn't going to be around forever. But that was before word of the gift got out. I suppose you know about that?"

"I would like your perspective."

"First I heard of the mess was when Keith called me at my office. He said news of the whole business had apparently leaked out, and that the school newspaper had run an interview with Markham in which that bastard said the university could do without my money, that I was a Commie, for God's sake. With serious issues like South Africa to be concerned about, that fugitive from the Stone Age was behaving like he was Joe McCarthy on one of his witch-hunts. Anyway, I was steamed, really steamed, and I told Keith that I wouldn't give a damn dime to the school, much as I loved it, as long as Markham was around. I told the campus paper the same thing when they called, too. And I meant it, by God."

"With Markham gone, have you reconsidered?"

Bach crossed his legs and looked into his glass, which was almost empty. "Confidentially, yes. Keith wants to wait a decent interval after Markham's death to trumpet it, though. Can't say I blame him."

"How does he define a decent interval?"

"Oh, about another month, but I think word is seeping out around the edges. It's pretty hard to keep anything quiet at a university, as I've been finding out. Now I'm going to guess one of your next questions," Bach said, leaning forward. "Where was I when Markham died? All right, what day was that?"

Wolfe turned to me, asking the question without speaking. "September twenty-third, late in the evening, or after midnight, which would have made it the twenty-fourth," I said.

"Where was I that day?" Bach asked, addressing Annette.

She pulled a leather book from her purse and unzipped it. "On the morning of the twenty-third, you were at a meeting with the Pacific Petroleum Company executive committee in Los Angeles," she replied in a businesslike drawl you could get used to liking. "You flew in the company plane that afternoon to Seattle, where you attended a dinner honoring Senator Beattie. You had breakfast in Seattle on the twenty-fourth with the publisher of the local newspaper, and then you flew back to New York, arriving here late in the afternoon."

"Actually, I got back after dark," Bach corrected. "I remember the trip now, Annette, thanks. Mr. Wolfe, plenty of people will vouch for my being at those events, not that it matters."

The phone rang, and I picked it up at my desk while Bach went on talking. It was Cortland, who was jabbering so fast I had to ask him to slow down. He did, and I took notes on what he was telling me, working to keep my face under control. After he finished, I thanked him and said we'd be back to him soon. He was all wound up and wanted to keep going, but it was obvious he had nothing more to contribute so I cut him off.

Because Wolfe can't read my shorthand—nobody can but me—I copied in English what Cortland had told me and got up, walking to Wolfe's desk and putting the sheet on his blotter. "That was Mr. Wilson," I told him, using one of our codes. "He thought you'd want to know about this."

". . . anyway," Bach continued, "I can't say that I'm sorry Markham is dead, but as far as murder, it seems to me that this whole thing is being dramatized. After all, who'd *really* want to kill him?"

"Apparently the same individual who pushed one of his students into Caldwell's Gash sometime today or tonight," Wolfe said sourly, holding the paper I'd just handed him. "The body of a young woman named Gretchen Frazier has been found at the precise spot where the corpse of Mr. Markham was discovered."

EIGHTEEN

"The hell you say!" Bach snapped upright at Wolfe's words, almost spilling what little water was left in his glass. "Somebody *else* is dead at Prescott?"

"So Mr. Goodwin just learned on the telephone." Wolfe's expression was grim. "The young woman who had been described as Mr. Markham's outstanding graduate student."

"When was she found? How did she die?"

"Our report is incomplete, although Mr. Goodwin may have something to add to the message he handed me."

"Not really," I said. "As Mr. Wolfe told you, Gretchen Frazier's body apparently was found not long ago at the bottom of Caldwell's Gash, right where Markham's body had been discovered. It appears that she, like Markham, went over the edge."

"That's hideous—it sounds like ritual killings." It was Annette Carswell, with shock in her soft drawl. She fastened her eyes on Wolfe and then on me, as if demanding an explanation.

"Whatever it is, that should end everyone's doubts as to whether Markham was murdered," I observed.

"Incredible," Bach said, his voice an octave higher. "This is a terrible thing for the school, damned terrible."

"And not so great for either Markham or Gretchen Frazier," I said.

"Oh, of course, of course, I didn't mean to sound

callous," the old tycoon put in quickly. "Who called you?" It was more like a demand than a question.

"A source whom Mr. Goodwin and I consider to be reliable," Wolfe snapped.

"All right, all right, I don't blame you for not wanting to answer. Confidentiality between practitioner and client and all that," Bach conceded. "I'll assume it's that professor that Keith Potter told me about—what's his name?—Cortland. The one who was such a close friend of Markham's and was sure he was murdered, so he paid you to find out. I don't know what you're charging him, but it can't be all that much, given faculty salaries. I'll triple whatever it is and hire you to do the same thing— find who killed both Markham and that girl. It must be the same person."

"What is your sudden interest?" Wolfe's eyes narrowed. "Just minutes ago, you were arguing that Markham's death wasn't murder."

"That was before we heard about the girl, and what happened must be more than a coincidence. Okay, it looks like you were right. As to why the interest, I've told you how I feel about Prescott. The longer these deaths go on unsolved without somebody getting nailed, the worse the school looks. Don't you agree?"

"I do, sir. As you have observed, though, I already am engaged in determining the truth. Do you feel that I would increase my efforts if my compensation were greater?"

"Money sets the world in motion." Bach clearly expected no argument on that.

"So Publilius Syrus wrote. And it would be fatuous of me to gainsay my fondness for monetary reward. However, changing clients in midcourse is a dubious practice for a number of reasons, most of which I'm sure you recognize and sympathize with."

Bach yanked at his tie and folded his arms across his chest. "Point taken. Well, regardless of who the client is, you're on this thing. Good. And so, I would hope, are the local cops."

"I won't presume to speak for them, sir," Wolfe said,

"but it seems likely they now will find themselves under considerable pressure."

"Hah—I should think so. Well, I'll take no more of your time; you've got more important things to do than to humor me," Bach said good-naturedly as he got to his feet. His personal assistant stood, too. Our eyes met and I smiled, but got nothing in return except a cool green glance. I walked them to the front hall and helped Annette with her coat while Bach, ever independent, tugged his own on hurriedly. "Mr. Goodwin," he said, shaking my hand firmly, "I hope Wolfe gets this thing untangled fast. I frankly don't put much stock in the Prescott police. Thanks for the drink and the hospitality. Good night." Annette shook hands, too, but only nodded after I warmly wished her a good evening. She might have done all right in the looks segment of a beauty pageant, but she would have washed out in the Miss Congeniality competition.

When I got back to the office after bolting the front door behind our guests, I found Wolfe sitting with his eyes closed. "Well, what now?" I asked. I got no answer, and after a full minute of silence I tried again.

"Okay, now I understand. We do nothing, right? We wait for the bodies to pile up at the bottom of Caldwell's Gash and eventually the only one left alive is the murderer, is that it? Sorry I'm so slow on the uptake. All that driving up to Prescott and back must have dulled my senses."

"So that's the explanation," Wolfe said, opening his eyes and glaring at the empty glass on his blotter. "I need beer."

"Normally I'd tell you to get it yourself, but I know the strain you've been under," I told him, pushing to my feet and heading for the kitchen. I returned with two chilled bottles and set them down in front of him. "Service with a smile," I said, returning to my desk the long way, via the makeshift bar, where I mixed myself another Scotch.

"Archie, you mentioned something earlier about

Markham having kept a log of the books he checked out of the library."

"I'll be damned, I didn't know you were listening. Yeah, I told you about his library books, his clothes, and his—"

"I'd like to see that list of books, please."

By that, Wolfe meant he wanted a printout. It would have been easier, of course, for me to simply pop the disk in and have him read it on the screen, but as I learned in the months we'd had the computer, he refused to use the terminal. He didn't trust anything that wasn't on the desk in front of him in black and white.

I briefly considered tweaking him again about this new idiosyncrasy, but checked myself. However strange the request, he actually was doing something. This was progress. I put the LIBRARY BOOKS disk into the computer and activated the printer, which chattered for a little under a minute, spitting out the list. I tore off the sheet of paper and walked it to Wolfe's desk, laying it in front of him with a mild flourish:

UNIVERSITY LIBRARY

TITLE	OUT	DUE	RETURNED
Conservatism from John Adams to Churchill	3–26	4–26	4–19
The Rage of Edmund Burke: Portrait of an Ambivalent Conservative	4–7	5–7	5–2
The Radical Right. The New American Right Expanded and Updated	7–17	8–17	8–19
An Historical Anthology of Select British Speeches	7–17	8–17	8–19

PUBLIC LIBRARY

TITLE	OUT	DUE	RETURNED
Reflections on the Revolution in France	6–24	7–24	7–23
The Future of Conservatism; from Taft to Reagan and Beyond	7–22	8–22	8–13
Ten North Frederick	8–16	9–16	9–14
Cass Timberlane	8–16	9–16	9–14
The Optimist's Daughter	8–21	9–21	9–18
Ideas in Conflict—The Political Theories of the Contemporary World	8–21	9–21	9–18

Wolfe studied the list, scowled, and tossed it aside. "His checking account now, please."

"Going to see if he wrote a check for those overdue books in August?" I asked. I began to suspect this was merely an exercise to keep me from harassing him. Or worse, maybe it was the only idea he had, and he was firing blindly, hoping to hit something. "Here's his check ledger since the first of the year," I said three minutes later, handing him another printout. "Balance as of last entry, eleven hundred ninety-six dollars, fifty-five cents. Do you want his other finances, too?"

Wolfe shook his head as he scanned the list of checks, then tossed it aside, too, and rose, heading for the door.

"That's it?" I asked. "No more printouts? No orders for me?"

"Archie, it is now eleven-thirty-five," he said, stopping in the doorway to the hall. "Tomorrow is soon enough to plan a course of action. Good night."

I started to call after him that it was never too soon to plan a course of action, but before I could get my phrasing just right, I heard the banging of the elevator door, followed by the whir of the motor as it labored to carry its load of a seventh of a ton upstairs.

I sat at my desk for several minutes, sipping the last

of the Scotch and pondering the day's events. A second death had been visited upon Prescott. A millionaire—or maybe he's a billionaire—had come to the house offering to pay triple the fee we were working on and got told thanks, but no thanks. And a beautiful woman looked right through me as though I were invisible. And after all this, the resident genius pulls a Scarlett O'Hara and tells me tomorrow is another day. Is it any wonder that I indulge myself in an occasional sip of something stronger than milk?

NINETEEN

I had an inkling that Monday would be more than a little hectic, and my inkle was right. I was in the kitchen attacking link sausage, scrambled eggs, muffins, and coffee at eight-fifteen when the phone rang. "It's Mr. Cohen," Fritz said, cupping the receiver. "He sounds excited."

"He always sounds excited; it's an occupational hazard. Tell him I'll call him as soon as I finish eating."

Fritz repeated my instructions into the phone, then listened and said "no" twice before hanging up. "He wasn't happy, Archie. He tried to get me to interrupt you while you were eating, but of course I would not do that."

"Of course. Fritz, I don't say this often enough—you are a gem." He blushed and turned his back to me as he went on with preparations for lunch. Fritz Brenner gets easily embarrassed by compliments, but don't think for a moment that he doesn't like to get them, whether they're about his cooking or anything else he does in the brownstone, which includes playing waiter, butler, housekeeper, phone answerer, and all-around indispensable man.

Lon undoubtedly had seen the story on Gretchen Frazier's death in the morning edition of the *Times*. Six paragraphs long, it was on page fourteen in the first section. It said her body was found at the bottom of Caldwell's Gash by two joggers a little after seven Sunday evening, which would have put it just about sunset. Death was attributed to "massive head injuries" apparently suffered in the 125-foot fall, according to the county medical examiner. The *Times* quoted Prescott Police Chief Carl Hobson as saying "Foul play has not been ruled out. We are investigating." And of course mention was made that Gretchen was an honors graduate student whose adviser, Hale Markham, had been found dead in similar circumstances in the same location a few weeks earlier. One further irony the paper pointed out: A fence along the rim of the Gash at the point where both Markham and Gretchen went over the edge was to have been installed today.

I dialed Lon and got him on the first ring. "Archie, what in the name of Mario Cuomo is happening up at Prescott? Don't think I've forgotten your supposedly innocuous call the other day. And then I pick up this morning's *Times* and read about that coed. Something tells me we're not talking coincidence here."

"Something tells me you're right, friend. I can't say much right now, mainly because I don't know much."

"And you call yourself a friend? Oh, come on, Archie. Give me something."

"Okay, but not for publication yet. If any of what I'm about to tell you gets into print now, I'll clam up later, when the real story develops, assuming there is one. Got it?"

"Got it," Lon said grimly.

"Okay, here's the picture, at least as much of it as I have: We have a client—name, Walter Cortland. The guy's a political science prof at Prescott and was a disciple of Markham's. And fiercely loyal to Markham, at least to hear him tell it.

"Anyway, Cortland called last Monday and came to see us Tuesday, saying he was sure Markham had been helped over the edge of that poor-man's Grand Canyon on the campus. He couldn't—or wouldn't—nominate anybody as the shover, though. To make a long story short, I've been up to Prescott three times, and Wolfe has even been there himself, and—"

"Wolfe went to Prescott?" Lon wheezed in disbelief.

"Don't interrupt—it's impolite. Yes, the man himself

got a taste of contemporary college life, and discovered, incredible as I know it must sound, that he likes the brownstone better. To continue, we talked to a number of people up there, including Gretchen Frazier. She was a student of Markham's, as this morning's *Times* points out, and it's also highly possible that their relationship was something more than just teacher and pupil. Several of the others we talked to were considerably less enthusiastic about him. As you recall, when I asked you about him a few days ago, you said he had a reputation for being irascible, contentious, and not exactly popular with other faculty members. With the exception of one woman in the History Department, your report seems accurate, based on our experience."

"It would be a woman," Lon remarked. "I'm not surprised, given his supposed reputation with the ladies."

"Uh-huh. At this point, Wolfe is mulling the situation over, at least I like to tell myself he is, but if he's getting ready to throw a net over someone, he isn't sharing it with me."

"That's it?" Lon asked.

"That's it for now. Film at eleven."

"Very funny. Okay, Archie, I'm good for my word—you know that. But when something happens, remember your old poker-playing buddy."

"How could I forget? The way I figure it, through the years, my contributions have probably paid for that knockout white fur I saw your wife wearing last winter." Lon answered with a word best omitted from this report, and I hung up, turning back to the *Times* piece on Gretchen, which I scissored out of the paper and slipped into the top center drawer of my desk. No sooner had I finished than the phone rang. It was Cortland, who sounded even more breathless than Lon.

"Mr. Goodwin, I've just returned home from police headquarters," he huffed. "They telephoned me early this morning and requested my presence—demanded it, actually. I asked if I could defer the visit until afternoon, but the man on the other end was adamant. He said someone could come for me in a car, and I told him 'No thank you.' After all, who wants a police vehicle pulling up in front of their house, especially with the meddlesome neighbors I've got? So I went on foot—it's only a little over four blocks. And do you know what transpired when I got there?"

"Sure. They grilled you."

"What? Oh—grilled. Interrogated. Yes, that's just what they did. And none too nicely, I'd like to tell you. There were two of them, a lieutenant named Powers and another cretin, and they bombarded me with a lot of rude questions about Gretchen Frazier and Hale. They even asked me if I'd ever been . . . *involved* with Gretchen, if you can conceive such outrageous affrontery!"

"Had you?"

"I'm afraid I don't find that the least bit humorous, Mr. Goodwin. The answer, of course, is no. The police also insisted on ascertaining where I was yesterday at the time they calculate that poor girl went into the Gash. I told them the truth, of course—that I was home alone."

Academics seem to spend a lot of time at home alone—when they're not bumping one another off. "When did they say that was?"

"Lieutenant Powers declared it was sometime between five-thirty and when she was found. I was at home every bit of that time."

"How did you find out last night that she had died?"

"I received a call around eight-thirty or so from Orville Schmidt. He said he had just learned from somebody, Campus Security, I believe it was. It's incredible how speedily word flies in a place like Prescott. Anyway, he said he was calling each faculty member in the department to tell them personally. He seemed understandably appalled and said this would be horrific for the department and the university."

"Sounds like Leander Bach," I said.

"What?"

"Nothing. What else did the police ask you?"

"What *didn't* they ask? They were obsessed in their desire to know how well Hale and Gretchen knew each other. As much as the question offended me, I said I thought she admired him as a great teacher and he was excited by her intellectual potential—both of which I firmly believe constituted the total basis of their friendship. They asked if Hale had enemies on campus, and I said I was aware of none, beyond the usual petty jealousies."

"Did you tell them about the feuds with Schmidt and Greenbaum? And the business with Potter and Bach over the bequest to the school?"

"I did," he said after several seconds. "Although they already knew about the Bach brouhaha because of all the commotion it generated at the time."

"How did the police leave things after they finished talking to you?"

"They told me to be available in the event that they needed to talk to me again. And they weren't very polite about that, either, I might add."

"Murder, or even the suspicion of murder, tends to make cops feisty," I said, "whether they're in New York or New Paltz. I wouldn't be too hard on them."

"They behaved rudely—boorishly," Cortland whimpered, "and I can't forgive that in anyone, let alone public employees. Our taxes are what pay their salaries, after all."

"I'm sure they get reminded of that often enough. But back to the subject at hand: Mr. Wolfe is at work, believe me. I'm confident that he's on the brink of solving this thing, and I'll keep you apprised of every development."

Cortland sounded doubtful as we said good-bye, and for that matter I was pretty doubtful myself. Lying to clients always bothered me for at least fifteen minutes after I did it, which probably reflects my small-town, middle-class Ohio origins.

If I *had* told Cortland the truth, it probably would have sounded something like this: "I'm terribly sorry, but Mr. Wolfe at present is not in the proper frame of mind to do any thinking about the problem for which you have engaged him and are paying handsomely. He has his orchids to worry about, and his reading—he's plowing through three books right now—and his crossword puzzles, not to mention the time he is forced to spend overseeing our chef, Mr. Brenner, to ensure that the proper types and amounts of seasonings and sauces are added to the gourmet dishes that comprise such a big part of Mr. Wolfe's life. So you can see that this doesn't leave a lot of time for detecting, which after all is something Mr. Wolfe only dabbles in, despite its being his primary source of income. I ask your patience in this matter, and I can assure you that Mr. Wolfe will get back to work on your problem soon, quite possibly as early as next week, but certainly no later than the week after that."

I was still mentally composing this spiel when Wolfe walked into the office at two minutes after eleven, eased his bulk into the desk chair after wishing me a curt good morning, and started in on the mail, which as usual I'd placed on his blotter. He was halfway through the stack when the doorbell rang.

I went to the hall and, seeing a familiar face through the one-way glass panel, returned to the office. "Cramer," I said. "Should I let him in?" Wolfe nodded and turned back to the mail.

"Hello, Inspector. What a surprise," I said, swinging the door open. "Nice morning, isn't it?"

"It'll do," he rumbled, barreling past me as he always does and making straight for the office. In all the years I've known Inspector Cramer of the New York Police Department's homicide detail, I can almost never remember his hanging up his overcoat or even handing it to me to hang up. I would have accused him of imitating Peter Falk except that he was around long before *Columbo* came along. Besides, whatever else I might say about Cramer, he is his own man and doesn't feel the need to imitate anybody, least of all a television cop.

"Good morning, Inspector," Wolfe said as Cramer let his 190 pounds drop into the red leather chair and took a cigar from his overcoat pocket. "I'm about to have beer. Will you join me?"

"Too early," he gruffed, chewing on the unlit stogie. "I'll only be a minute. I got a call first thing this morning from the police chief in Prescott—name's Hobson, as I guess you know. He claims we met at a law enforcement conference years ago, although I sure as hell don't remember it. He wanted to know all about you."

"And?" Wolfe raised his eyebrows.

"He said you and Goodwin had been up in Prescott investigating that professor's death," Cramer snorted. "I said I didn't believe him—that there was no way you'd be caught that far from the city, but he insisted it was you and described you to the letter. Then I told him I'd known you for more years than I care to count, that you're one shrewd cookie, that you've figured out a lot of tough cases, and that sometimes I trust you, sometimes I don't. I also told him that when you give your word on something, it can be taken to the bank, but you're as mule-headed as anybody he'd ever find."

"Mr. Cramer, I have always admired your candor," Wolfe said, pouring beer into a glass from one of the two bottles Fritz had just set in front of him.

"Yeah. Well, I didn't come over here just to butter you up," Cramer muttered, gesturing with his cigar. "The way I read it, what with this client of yours that Hobson told me about, you're getting ready to nail somebody for giving the big push to both the professor and the girl. Okay, that's your affair and technically it belongs to those folks up in Orange County. But I've been around you long enough to know that whenever you hold one of your overblown charades and gather everybody in this room for the big moment, the murderer is always sitting there along with everybody else. So whether or not you ask any police from Prescott to come, this is part of my turf, and I intend to be right here." Cramer jabbed his chest with his finger and bit into his cigar as if it were a medium-rare filet.

"If such an event occurs, you assuredly will be invited," Wolfe said, turning a palm over. "I wouldn't think of omitting you—or Sergeant Stebbins—from the guest list."

Cramer eyed Wolfe suspiciously, took one last chew of the battered panatela, and slowly got to his feet. "I just can't believe you went to Prescott," he said, shaking his head. "Were you unconscious all the way up and back?"

I'm happy to report that Wolfe ignored that cheap shot and reached for the mail again while Cramer turned on his heel and marched out to the front hall with me close behind. "You may have hurt Mr. Wolfe's feelings with your last comment," I said to his back, but got no answer as he stalked out and went down our front steps to the unmarked car at the curb.

"Nice of Cramer to stop by, eh?" I said back in the office. "Like old times." Wolfe grunted and I filled him in on the earlier calls from Lon and Cortland. He finished perusing the mail and looked up. "Is Mr. Cortland where he can be reached?"

"I can try," I shrugged. "You want him now?"

Wolfe nodded and I dialed his office number, getting my favorite new girlfriend. "Yes, he's here, Mr. Goodman," she chirped, instantly recognizing my voice, which warmed my heart. "Hold on, please."

I signaled to Wolfe, who picked up his receiver while I stayed on the line. "Mr. Cortland, this is Nero Wolfe—" Before he could get any more out, Cortland loudly bemoaned his morning at the police station, railing at the manners and methods of Prescott's finest. He was in good form, I had to admit. Wolfe made a face as he listened, mouthing an occasional sympathetic word. "Sir," he said after our client had finally wound down, "if I may presume on your time for just a few moments, I have a question: Was Mr. Markham a reader of fiction?"

"Hale? Almost never," Cortland said. "He thought it was a waste of time. So do I, for that matter. In fact, now that you mention it, I can't ever remember hearing him talk about a novel. Why in the world do you ask?"

Wolfe ducked the question and thanked him, cradling the receiver and leaning back in his chair, eyes closed. I knew what was coming before it started, don't ask me how—maybe I've just been around him so long that I unconsciously pick up the signals. After about a minute, it began—his lips pushing out and in, out and in. I never know where he is at these times and I doubt if he knows himself. Because I've gotten into the habit through the years, I timed him as he sat there doing the lip drill. After a few seconds more than twenty-two minutes by my watch, he opened his eyes, blinked twice, and sat up straight. "Confound it, let's be done with this," he grumbled. "Get all of them here."

"You mean right now?"

"Tonight will be soon enough. I suggest nine o'clock."

"Oh, what a relief—then there'll be no problem. After all, that's almost ten hours away. But will you be kind enough to define 'all of them' for me?"

"I would have thought that patently obvious," he said dryly. "Messrs. Potter, Greenbaum, Schmidt, and Bach, and Mrs. Moreau. And our client, of course. Also, that cretinous police chief from Prescott."

"So you *are* inviting the billionaire. You realize that means you'll also be getting his personal assistant in the package?"

Wolfe nodded, returning to the beer he'd abandoned during his séance.

"And you promised Inspector Cramer a seat at the proceedings, too."

"I will call Mr. Cramer," Wolfe replied. "After lunch is soon enough."

"Assuming everybody shows up, this place is going to be more crowded than a room filled with Johnny Carson's guest hosts."

"I have absolute confidence in your ability to work out the logistics." Wolfe turned to an orchid growers' magazine. I picked up on that signal, too—it meant the discussion was officially over, but that was all right with me, because things were about to get interesting.

TWENTY

After getting my marching orders, I turned immediately to the telephone and started in to deliver on those orders. I caught Cortland in his office just as he was leaving for lunch. "Mr. Wolfe is going to make an announcement here tonight," I told him. "You're invited, of course, and so are Potter, Schmidt, Greenbaum, and Mrs. Moreau."

"What information is he going to impart?"

"I don't know," I replied honestly. "Except that I think it's fair to say you'll all want to hear it."

"May I please speak with Mr. Wolfe?" he asked, the peevishness still in his voice.

"Sorry, he's not available right now." Okay, so that's twice in this narrative that I've lied to a client. There was a long pause at the other end.

"All right," Cortland sighed, "I'll be present."

"Think you can get the others?"

Another pause. "I drew them together once for you—isn't that sufficient?"

"Look, Mr. Cortland, you wanted Mr. Wolfe to take this case—begged him, in fact, through me. And now it looks like you just might be getting some results. It seems to me you'd want to do everything you could to help things along. After all, you *are* the client."

Yet another pause followed by another sigh. "You're right," he finally said. "And I am happy to learn of progress. It's just that my colleagues here are highly irritated with me by now, as I'm sure you can appreciate.

But I'll ask them—in fact, I will probably be encountering at least some of them over in the Union at lunch."

As a sign-off I gave him a few words of encouragement and told him to let me know the results, then swiveled to face Wolfe. "I don't know if you heard that or not, but Cortland's trying to round up the college crowd. Should I invite his eminence the police chief of Prescott, or would you prefer to do the honors?"

Wolfe set his book down and scowled. "You do it. If he balks, I'll get on the line."

A female voice answered at the Prescott police station, and when I told her I wanted to talk to Chief Hobson, she put me through without even bothering to ask my name. There are some advantages to dealing with small-town institutions after all.

"Carl Hobson," he answered gruffly.

"Mr. Hobson, this is Archie Goodwin. You recall we met the other day. I'm calling for Mr. Wolfe, who is inviting you to a meeting at his house in New York tonight at nine o'clock. He plans to—"

"Me? Come to New York? What the hell kind of a game is this?"

"I started to say that he plans to name the murderer of both Hale Markham and Gretchen Frazier, and—"

"Goddamn it, let me talk to Wolfe!"

I cupped the receiver. "He would very much like to speak to you," I told Wolfe. "And he's not being a gentleman about it."

Wolfe gave me one of his looks of resignation and picked up his instrument. "Yes, Mr. Hobson?" he said nonchalantly.

"What is this claptrap about a meeting at your place to name a murderer?"

"Mr. Goodwin described it accurately. I thought you would relish the opportunity to be present."

"Inspector Cramer told me about your methods, Mr. Wolfe. Things down in New York may be run casually, but we don't operate that way in Prescott. Whatever it is you plan to say tonight, you can spit it out right now."

"No, sir, that won't work. What I have to say I will say here—and only here—tonight."

"If you think I'm going to drive all the way down there—and to a meeting about possible homicides, in a private home at that—you're badly mistaken," Hobson snarled.

"Suit yourself, sir," Wolfe said. "Whether you come or not, law enforcement will be represented in the person of Inspector Cramer."

Hobson swore and then cupped his receiver while he talked to someone else. I couldn't make out any of it. "What's your address?" he barked when he came back on the line. Wolfe told him and the chief growled that he would see if he could arrange to come.

My next call was to Leander Bach's office, and again I went through the switchboard. This time, however, when I gave my name and got passed on to Bach's office, the call went directly to Annette Carswell. "Yes, Mr. Goodwin?" came the ten-degree-Fahrenheit voice.

I repeated basically the same speech I'd given Hobson. "Mr. Bach is at home this morning, but I expect him in the office later," she replied. "If he decides to come—and I stress the *if*—he'll probably ask me to accompany him."

"Fine with us," I told her, and we left it that she'd call to let me know one way or the other.

"Eight-to-five he shows," I said to Wolfe. "Cramer next?" My answer was a nod, so I dialed the number I know by heart, and Wolfe picked up his phone when Cramer came on the line. "Inspector, I didn't realize I would be calling you this soon after your visit. You said you wanted an invitation to my next . . . I believe 'charade' is the term you used. It will be tonight at nine o'clock."

"I'll be damned," Cramer murmured. "Who else is coming?"

Wolfe recited the list, including Hobson. "Sergeant Stebbins of course is also welcome," Wolfe said, but all he got in return from Cramer was another "I'll be damned" before he said he'd be there and hung up.

* * *

We were back in the office after lunch with our coffee when the next installment came—in the form of a call from the president of Prescott University. "Mr. Wolfe, I saw Walter Cortland a few minutes ago, and he informed me of your gathering tonight," Potter said. "I'm afraid I won't be able to accept because of a previous commitment."

"I would strongly advise you to rearrange your schedule," Wolfe murmured, closing his eyes.

"When you're in my position, that's not always easy to do," was the stiff reply.

"I appreciate that, sir. But I naturally assumed, given the impact these recent events have had on the university and its image, that you might want to be present. I am expecting several of your faculty to attend."

Potter probably thought he was too refined to swear, but I know he was itching to. He, too, paused, and then muttered something about seeing if he couldn't postpone a meeting. He asked for the time and the address, and when he got them, he hung up.

"I'll give nine-to-five on that one," I said. "Now all we have to do is hear back from Cortland."

"You will receive a call from him in the next hour," Wolfe said, "and he will tell you that they are all coming, although both Mr. Schmidt and Mr. Greenbaum howled loudly about it, and Mr. Schmidt at first flatly refused to come. He also will tell you Mrs. Moreau reacted far more positively, agreeing almost immediately to come."

"Pretty smug, aren't you? Well, I don't want to bet against you because I'm hoping all of them show, but it would serve you right if they didn't follow your script. A little humility would be a healthy thing for you."

"Archie, too often what we refer to as humility is only false modesty strutting on the parade ground."

"Very nice. Who said it?"

"I did," Wolfe replied, returning to his book.

At three-twenty-five, Cortland called, and I was glad Wolfe wasn't listening in. "Mr. Goodwin, I spoke to all of them. Orville and Ted really bridled about making the trip to Manhattan, and Orville insisted, rather violently, if you must know, that he was remaining at home, but they both eventually calmed down and said they will be in attendance—in fact, we probably all will drive in together. Elena was more matter-of-fact about coming—she'll be there, too. I'm not so convinced about Keith; he became testy when I told him and said he was going to call you— did he?"

"Almost an hour ago. He was wrestling with himself, but I think we can count on him showing up."

"Mr. Goodwin," Cortland said anxiously, "is there anything I should be aware of beforehand?"

"Nope. Other than the fact that the office is going to be pretty crowded. See you at nine." It was obvious he wanted to talk some more, but I told him I had work to do and politely got rid of him. At least I like to think I was polite.

"Okay, you were more or less right about the Prescott crowd; they're all coming," I said to Wolfe. "Now it's time for you to open up. I think I may have it partly figured, but I admit I'm still groping. Let me tell you how I see it." I then proceeded to give him my theory, which turned out to be in the ballpark, although I was missing a few pieces that Wolfe supplied and that you may well have spotted some time back in this narrative. He got done laying it out for me just in time to take the northbound elevator to the plant rooms at four o'clock, leaving me to begin planning for the evening's activities.

First, though, I called Lon Cohen. "It's your old buddy, your old pal," I told him. "Wolfe is going to dump the whole thing out here tonight, and unless one of them blabs afterward, none of the A.M. papers will have time to glom on to any of it before you do."

"What can you give me now?" Lon never gives up.

"Nothing, I'm afraid. But I promise I'll call you as soon as the dust clears here tonight. If I had to guess, it would be some time around eleven, maybe eleven-thirty."

"Come on, Archie, let a little of it out now so I can begin working on assembling all this. Otherwise I'll probably be at it all night."

"Sorry, no can do. But when you get it, you'll get the whole package, and all I ask is that you spruce your layout of it up with photos of the legendary detectives Nero Wolfe and Archie Goodwin."

Before he hung up, Lon said something, and it wasn't "thank you."

TWENTY-ONE

Because Wolfe doesn't like turmoil in the office when he's ensconced there reading, drinking beer, or otherwise finding ways to occupy himself, Fritz and I did the setting up for the evening while he was upstairs playing with his plants. We moved in chairs from the dining room and front room—enough to accommodate everybody on the guest list plus a second policeman from Prescott. Cops always seem to travel in pairs, just like the nuns back home when I was a kid.

Fritz has firm ideas on how a bar should be stocked, and they include carafes of both white and red wine, even though I've been telling him for years that nobody drinks red wine except at meals where red meat is served. "No, Archie, it is proper that red should be there, too," he always insists, and in the interest of domestic tranquility, I invariably concede the point. When we were finished, Fritz slipped back to the kitchen to work on dinner— onion soup, beef Wellington, and cherry cobbler—and I went up to my room to shave and put on a fresh shirt. After all, we were having guests later in the evening, and nothing makes a worse impression than a twelve-hour growth, regardless of the grooming habits of certain prime-time TV stars.

At dinner, Wolfe held forth on the American penal system, which he contended has succeeded only in increasing the number of people in the prisons while failing abysmally as an instrument for rehabilitation. I lobbed in a comment here and there but mainly listened and consumed three helpings of the beef Wellington, plus seconds on the cherry cobbler. When we went back to the office for coffee, Fritz came in with a message: A Miss Carswell had called while we were eating to say that she and Mr. Bach would be joining us at nine. "There's my eight-to-five shot coming home," I told Wolfe, but he seemed more interested in an article on vanda hybrids in his new orchid magazine, so I moved over to the computer and fiddled with the germination records to kill time.

When the doorbell rang at eight-fifty-three, I made a bet with myself that it was Cramer. Sure enough, through the one-way panel I saw the impassive faces of the inspector and Sergeant Purley Stebbins. "Gentlemen," I greeted them formally, opening the door and stepping aside. "You're the first ones here; go right on into the office." I got a nod from Purley, an honest, tough cop whom I've known, respected, and fought with for years, and who may respect me as well, although I know he thinks I can't always be trusted. I got a snarl from Cramer, who in the right circumstances would snarl at his own mother. I started to follow them into the office, but before I could get there the bell sounded again. This was the Prescott faculty contingent: Cortland, Schmidt, Greenbaum, and Elena Moreau, all of them, even Elena, looking like they'd rather be someplace—anyplace—else.

I wished the quartet a good evening, taking coats, hanging them on the pegs in the hallway, and reserving a smile for Elena, who was wearing a businesslike cinnamon-colored dress that made me appreciate her sense of fashion. "How long will this take?" Greenbaum demanded. "A lot of us have got morning classes, you know, and we'll be lucky to be back home before midnight." I said something about how Wolfe doesn't like to waste time and then ushered the professors into the office, where I introduced them to Cramer and Stebbins while Wolfe looked on.

"New York police here?" Schmidt said, eyebrows raised. "May I ask why, Mr. Wolfe?"

"They are here at my invitation. Inspector Cramer

heads the New York Police Department's Homicide Squad, and tonight's discussion patently will be about homicide."

Schmidt started to yap, but he was interrupted by the doorbell, and this time I let Fritz get it while I took drink orders. Elena and Schmidt each asked for Scotch-and-water, while Cortland politely declined and Greenbaum snarled a "no." I was handing drinks out when the new arrivals entered: Leander Bach and Annette Carswell, followed by Keith Potter. Bach, wearing another pricey pinstripe, shook hands with the others, while Potter, whose own suit was hardly shabby, put on a ceremonial smile, nodded to his colleagues, and stiffly greeted Cramer and Stebbins. Annette, looking fetching in a blue dress with a wide white collar, stayed discreetly in the background, which seemed to be her ongoing role with Bach.

I had the chairs arranged in three rows and after a signal from Wolfe shifted to my task as usher. Bach got the red leather chair at the end of Wolfe's desk, with Annette on his left in one of the yellow chairs. Filling out the front row were Potter on Annette's left and Elena closest to me, also in yellow chairs. Behind them were Greenbaum, who was farthest from me, with Schmidt on his left and Cortland behind Elena. The back row of four chairs moved in from the dining room was reserved for the police. Stebbins was closest to me, with Cramer on his right and two vacant spots in the corner for the big cheese from Prescott and anybody he might bring along.

Wolfe eyed the empty chairs and turned to me. I shrugged, and just then the bell rang again. "I'll take it," I said, and got to the hall in time to see Fritz opening the front door for Carl Hobson and another man, whom I recognized as the surly Lieutenant Powers. "We've been waiting for you," I told them as Fritz took their coats. "But you'll be happy to know we haven't started yet." Those words didn't make them look the least bit happy, but I smiled anyway and directed them to the office. "Here are the last of our guests," I announced cheerfully as we entered, and I introduced them around while they moved to the remaining seats, nodding to Cramer and Stebbins.

"I don't believe this!" Greenbaum sputtered. "There are now four policemen in this room, in a private home, apparently in an unofficial capacity, and there's supposedly a lunatic killer among us, too—or at least that's what we've been led to believe. This is bizarre!"

"Mr. Greenbaum, please," Wolfe said, holding up a palm. "To expand on what I said earlier, before everyone had arrived, the members of these two police departments are here at my invitation and remain at my sufferance. If there is indeed a murderer present, as you suggest, I should think you would be happy to have law enforcement officers at the ready."

"What I don't understand is why we're even *here* if this is a police matter," Greenbaum persisted, getting white.

"Let me make a suggestion," Cramer rasped from the back of the room. "I've been at these things before. Wolfe says he has the answer to the deaths of two people. Maybe he does, and maybe he doesn't, but I'm willing to hear what he has to say as long as it doesn't take too long."

"It will not take an inordinate amount of time, Inspector." Wolfe's eyes moved around the room, stopping briefly at each face. "In fact, I think all of you will be surprised by the brevity of this gathering." He stopped to pour beer and watch the foam settle before continuing. "As you all surely know, I was hired by Mr. Cortland to investigate Mr. Markham's death, which he held was murder."

"And which has now been borne out," Cortland cut in, waving his right arm. Greenbaum started to mutter again, and you could see that Schmidt was getting ready to jump in, mouth-first.

"If you please," Wolfe said, readjusting his bulk and showing his displeasure at the interruption with a frown. "There was nothing initially to indicate in any way that Mr. Markham was slain, is that correct, sir?" He directed his question at Hobson.

The chief cleared his throat and looked around uneasily, as if intimidated by the combined mental horsepower of the gathering. "That's right," he said huskily.

"What did your men think of the branches at the top of the Gash where Mr. Markham began his fall?"

"Uh, they were . . . broken—that is, some of them were."

"Indeed. Cleanly?"

"I don't know. That is, I think so."

"You think so. But you don't know." Wolfe's tone was faintly mocking. He was sticking it to Hobson for the jerking around he got up in Prescott. If I were a nobler person, I might have felt sorry for the country cop, but I was enjoying every second.

Wolfe dismissed Hobson with a glare. "The Prescott police and most of the rest of you here seemed comfortable with the medical examiner's ruling of accidental death. Further buttressing this position, Mrs. Moreau told Mr. Goodwin that the professor had had occasional fainting spells in recent months. Clearly, one such spell could have resulted in the fatal plunge into Caldwell's Gash during one of his evening constitutionals through the area called Old Oaks." My eyes went to Elena, who appeared to be having a hard time getting comfortable in her chair.

"But Mr. Cortland persisted in his belief that the fall had not been an accident," Wolfe continued. "I must admit that early on, I demurred, despite Mr. Goodwin's cajoling, and I accepted the commission primarily to humor him. I now confess publicly that he—along with Mr. Cortland—was correct and I was wrong."

"Okay, so you're human," Cramer piped up. "Believe it or not, some of us knew that a long time ago. I thought you said this was going to be brief."

"And so it will be, sir," Wolfe replied, "but just as you and the other law officers are here to learn the identity of a murderer, I am here to earn a fee. Mr. Cortland, am I proceeding at too slow a pace?"

"No—not at all," the professor said, blinking and looking surprised that his opinion was asked.

"Very well. It did not take me long to discover that Hale Markham was a magnet for animosity. Based on what I learned about the man, it was not inconceivable that someone might indeed have wanted him dead. There were—"

"Just a moment, please." It was Keith Potter, sitting upright and squaring the shoulders of his gray glen plaid. "Would you care to clarify that last statement?"

"I would not," Wolfe said coldly. "As I started to say, there were a number of people who had reason to wish him ill. For instance, there was you, Mr. Potter. Your dream of a large grant from Mr. Bach apparently had been dashed by Markham. And—"

"That's slanderous!" Potter roared. He got halfway out of his chair but sat down with a thud when Wolfe's open palm hit the top of his desk.

"I cannot prevent you from leaving," Wolfe told the president, "but I can stop your interruptions. Another outburst and I will instruct Mr. Goodwin to remove you from the room. I assure you that would be an easy task for him; he has dealt effectively with individuals far larger and more formidable than you." I puffed out my chest to show that Wolfe knew whereof he spoke while Potter, his ears crimson, slid down in his chair.

"Mr. Potter was not alone," Wolfe went on. "Mr. Bach, too, had felt Hale Markham's vitriol. Before I go on, do *you* wish to quarrel with that statement?" he asked, turning to the tycoon.

Leander Bach smiled and tilted his head to one side. "Can't quarrel with it," he said, scratching his chin. "By all means charge ahead. This is interesting. I'm glad I came."

"Thank you. Mr. Bach had been embarrassed—and angered—by Mr. Markham's violent public denunciation of his prospective gift, which was said to have been easily the largest in the university's history. Their quarrel was public knowledge, given that it was carried on largely in the columns of the campus newspaper. Less public were the differences between Mr. Markham and Messrs. Schmidt and Greenbaum."

"Do we have to go through this again?" It was Orville Schmidt, shaking his big head so vigorously that his double chins jiggled.

"I'm merely reviewing the situation for everyone's benefit," Wolfe said. "You, sir, were openly antagonistic to Hale Markham and he to you. He resented your getting the post of department chairman and you resented his success and recognition nationally as an author and celebrity."

"Celebrity? Aren't you indulging in hyperbole?" Schmidt asked, his bushy white eyebrows climbing halfway up his forehead.

"Perhaps, but he clearly was better known than anyone else at the school. Wouldn't you agree, Mr. Potter?"

The president passed a hand over his sculptured black hair. "I suppose so, although he worked at getting personal publicity harder than anyone else, too."

"Just so. One might go so far as to call him a publicity hound, which no doubt further irritated a number of his colleagues. Back to you, Mr. Schmidt: Is it not true that Mr. Markham went out of his way to harass and even humiliate you in staff meetings and on other public occasions?"

"You know damn well it's true," Schmidt muttered. "We've been over this once already."

"Further," Wolfe said, "Mr. Markham had read an advance copy of your new book and claimed to locate several passages that were—"

"That bastard!" Schmidt lunged to his feet, his face redder than the hue of a strawberry. "I knew he'd go around blabbing about that. Even after he told me . . ."

"Told you he wouldn't say anything?" Wolfe completed the sentence. "Why don't you inform the rest of us as to what this is about?"

Schmidt was back in his chair, looking like a deflated

balloon. He shook his head several times before beginning. "God knows how many people he shot his mouth
off to. Yes, Hale had read my book, and yes, he accused
me of plagiarism. Every scholarly book uses other
sources, of course. I have hundreds of footnotes, and
while I may have done some paraphrasing without
footnoting, it was—oh, dammit, why should I have to
defend myself? Everybody knows he had it in for me. He
was going to try to make me look bad any way he could.
That was the kind of man he was." He shook his head
again, eyes down, and the room was so quiet you could
hear the wall clock ticking.

"Very well. Mr. Greenbaum," Wolfe said, shifting
slightly to face his new target, "you and Hale Markham
had been close, very close, at one time, but several years
ago you left the conservative camp and in so doing
incurred Mr. Markham's lasting enmity. For that matter,
your feelings toward him were no less hostile."

"To echo Orville, we've been through this before."
Greenbaum was perched on the front quarter of his chair
as though he expected to jump up and bolt from the
room at any moment. My eyes left him and went to Elena
Moreau, who was looking at her hands clenched in her
lap. She had been in that pose for several minutes.

"From good friends, you and Mr. Markham shifted
to being antagonists," Wolfe continued, "spurred by his
feeling that you had sold out to the left to further your
academic career."

"I don't have to put up with any more of this bilge!"
Greenbaum yelled, standing and taking a step toward the
door.

"Sit down!" It was Cramer, who like Wolfe knew how
to get maximum inpact out of words without having to
shout. Greenbaum turned. "I don't have to listen to you,
either," he said, shaken. "You are not here on official
business—Wolfe said so."

Cramer didn't waver. "Sit down and shut up. I'll tell
you when it's time to go."

Greenbaum sat, and I wondered who would ask for
permission to leave next.

Wolfe went on. "Each of you gentlemen"—he looked in turn at Potter, Bach, Schmidt, and Greenbaum—"by words and/or actions, has shown that you had little use for Hale Markham. And all of you excepting Mr. Bach, who said he was on the West Coast, could conceivably have been at the rim of Caldwell's Gash with Mr. Markham on the night of September twenty-third."

"Just a minute," Potter said. "I told you before that I—"

"I said you conceivably could have been there. I don't think any of you were," Wolfe said. "In fact, until Miss Frazier was found at the bottom of the Gash, I foolishly questioned whether *anyone* had given Mr. Markham the fatal push, despite Mr. Goodwin's observation that the branches at the point where he fell were broken off cleanly. Such breaks of course are the kind a body being shoved would likely cause, rather than a body falling as deadweight.

"It took Miss Frazier's death to change my thinking, but even then, my brain moved with the speed of a tortoise. From the beginning, I recognized that Mr. Markham had not died as the result of a premeditated act; he either accidentally stumbled—the alternative I first favored—or he was pushed by someone in a moment of passion. It was clear to me that each of you gentlemen harbored animus toward him of such a nature that, had you decided to eliminate him, you surely would have done it in a calculated and well-planned manner rather than with a haphazard push, a push that might have resulted in his only being injured."

"Look out!" Purley Stebbins shouted, moving forward in a blur and reaching over Elena Moreau's shoulder from behind to grab her hand, which had gone into her purse. As she recoiled, he yanked her arm out, spilling the contents of the purse on the carpet. She was clutching something. "It's only this," she cried, holding an envelope up for everyone to see, and as she did so, Purley triumphantly snatched it from her hand.

"I was about to give it to Mr. Wolfe," she hissed, eyes blazing. "What are you trying to do to me?"

"I figured she was going for a gun or a knife," Purley said sheepishly to Cramer, who now was also on his feet. Everybody else was jabbering.

"Sergeant, I'll take that," Wolfe said. After another glance at Cramer, who nodded, Purley reached over and set the crumpled envelope on Wolfe's blotter, then retreated to his place in the back row.

Wolfe considered the envelope, then pushed it aside unopened. "To continue," he said, "Miss Frazier's death convinced me that Mr. Markham had indeed been murdered. The truth should have been apparent the instant I learned the circumstances of her demise, but"—he spread his hands, palms up—"I refused to read the signs. It took Mr. Goodwin's tenacity to awaken me. As some of you probably know, Mr. Markham was a most meticulous record keeper; using his personal computer, he cataloged virtually every facet of his life. Mr. Goodwin found that one of his myriad lists consisted of books he had checked out, from both the public and university libraries in Prescott. Most of them, not surprisingly, dealt with some aspect of political theory or theorists, but there were three novels—"

"That explains your question to me yesterday," Cortland interjected, stroking his chin.

Wolfe nodded. "Mr. Cortland informed me that Mr. Markham never read fiction, which was one reason these entries seemed curious. The other was the novels themselves: *Cass Timberlane*, by Sinclair Lewis; *The Optimist's Daughter*, by Eudora Welty; and *Ten North Frederick*, by John O'Hara. Do they suggest a pattern?"

Wolfe's eyes again swept the room. Elena shrugged, Greenbaum shook his head in puzzlement, and the others returned Wolfe's look with blank expressions. "Each of these books in varying degree and detail deals with romance and in some cases marriage involving a middle-aged or elderly man and a woman considerably his junior," he said. He was clearly enjoying himself.

"At the time of his death, Mr. Markham had particularly close friendships with two women—Gretchen Frazier and Mrs. Moreau, both far younger than he. I do not pretend to know the intimate details of these relationships, nor do I care to. But one of these liaisons clearly was on his mind, as evidenced by his interest in the novels. He had been close to Mrs. Moreau for some years, while Miss Frazier had been a recent arrival in his life. Patently, it was the latter who had been occupying his thoughts of late.

"I now shift to Miss Frazier's death," Wolfe said, draining the beer from his glass and dabbing his lips with the corner of a handkerchief. "The location is significant: the precise spot where the professor had plunged to his death more than three weeks earlier. Miss Carswell, when you and Mr. Bach were here last night and we received the news about Miss Frazier, you said it sounded like ritual killings."

Having the spotlight hit her startled Ms. Cool. "Why, yes—I guess I did," she said, straightening her back and looking around the room self-consciously. "When two people die the same way in the same place, that's what you naturally think of."

"Indeed. And the next thing likely to enter one's mind is why the second victim happened to be at the spot where the first death occurred."

"You know, that's been bugging me since last night," Leander Bach said, waggling a finger. "How could anyone have gotten her to show up there after what had happened before?"

"No one lured her, sir," Wolfe replied. "She went of her own free will."

"You can't possibly know that." It was Cramer.

"But I can—as surely as if I were present. Had someone schemed to draw Miss Frazier to that spot in the Old Oaks, she would not have taken the bait; only a fool is led willingly to destruction, and she was no fool."

"You're talking in circles," Schmidt growled. "And all the while, here we sit with a murderer."

"There is no murderer present," Wolfe contradicted, eyeing his empty glass. "I should think the truth would be obvious to all of you by now. Miss Frazier's death was indeed a ritual one, but it was of her own making: She hurled herself into the canyon."

TWENTY-TWO

Over the years I've heard some noise in Wolfe's office, but these college types really broke the Guinness decibel record. Everybody started yammering at once, to one another and at Wolfe. They all had something to say, most of them loudly and with as many syllables as possible, and for a good two minutes, the room sounded like the trading floor of the New York Stock Exchange. Wolfe leaned back and watched, trying to look grumpy, but he didn't fool me; he loves dropping bombs.

Cramer finally made his bark heard over the din. "Okay, you've had your fun. I hate to be the one to spoil the party, but there's no way you can prove your little scenario, Wolfe."

"Correct," Wolfe said, lacing his hands over his middle and waiting for the audience to sit down and calm down. When he had their attention, he went on. "With your forbearance, I will reconstruct the events as I believe them to have occurred. First and most basic, Miss Frazier was clearly enamored of her teacher and mentor, a man known for his interest in comely women. Despite the two-generation disparity in their ages, there was a mutual attraction. But not, I suspect, mutual affection. The young woman, likely dazzled by the attentions of a renowned figure—and one whose philosophies she shared and admired—was an easy prey. To the professor, it was just another conquest, however, and—"

"I don't believe it!" Cortland shrilled.

"Hear me out," Wolfe said sharply. "Mr. Goodwin, who met Miss Frazier on two occasions, contends that the intensity of her feelings for Mr. Markham was palpable. And I assure you that Mr. Goodwin's perspicacity in this area cannot be overestimated. It is my conviction that during the last few months Miss Frazier sought a permanent union with the professor—perhaps through marriage, although not necessarily. The subject of their relationship clearly was on his mind, as witness the books he had been reading, but he was not inclined to make any sort of commitment. Whether or not Mr. Markham had toyed with her affections is moot. Undoubtedly quarrels ensued, and the whole business came to a head on September twenty-third. At the edge of the Gash, Miss Frazier intercepted her mentor—or possibly met him by prearrangement—during his nightly constitutional, making one final effort to forge a permanent bond. But he was adamant. Feeling betrayed and used, she lost control and gave him a shove, sending him to his death. Being a dance instructor, she was likely both strong and agile, despite her size, and could easily have caught him off-balance. As to whether she meant to kill him . . . that likely will never be known."

"It sounds too pat to me." Chief Hobson was smirking. "Like maybe you're weaving a story to justify collecting your fat fee from Mr. Cortland here."

Wolfe looked blandly at the Prescott chief and stretched his arms in front of him, palms down on the blotter. "As I conceded earlier, there is no way I can prove my reconstruction, but Miss Frazier's subsequent death would seem to buttress it. What she had done naturally weighed heavily upon the young woman, although the horror that gripped her immediately following the act was replaced by a more abiding fear, that of being found out. After more than two weeks passed, however, she probably felt secure. After all, the county medical examiner's ruling had gone unchallenged, and life on the campus returned to normal. Then Mr. Goodwin and I materialized, and she quickly became aware that the accidental-death entry on the death certificate did not hold water with us.

"When I talked to the young woman just four days ago in Prescott, a delitescent panic was suggested by her demeanor, and when I asked her an elemental question—where was she on the night of Markham's death?—she promptly burst into tears, using this contrivance in the hopes of focusing my attention on her grief rather than on the question." What Wolfe omitted, in case you didn't notice, is that Gretchen's "contrivance" was sufficient to send him scurrying from the room.

"I firmly believe that during our conversation Miss Frazier came to the realization the game would soon be up," he continued. "How long she agonized before opting to destroy herself one can only guess, but I suspect she had settled the matter within forty-eight hours. And her decision to perish at the same place where Mr. Markham died bespeaks a sense of high tragedy."

"What about a suicide note?" Cramer asked, turning to Hobson.

"Nothing was found in her apartment," the chief said smugly. "We gave the place a good going-over this morning—I was there myself—and we didn't find anything that would link her to Markham. The only letters we found were from her parents."

"Okay, let's see what it was this lady had in her purse," Cramer growled, gesturing toward Elena.

Wolfe reached for the envelope that had been all but forgotten in the hubbub and drew out a single sheet, unfolding it deliberately and letting it rest in the palm of one hand. "Do I have your permission to share this?" he asked Elena. She nodded, tight-lipped.

"Archie," he said, sliding the paper across the desk toward me, "please read it aloud."

"It's a letter on peach-colored stationery, handwritten," I said, holding the sheet up by one corner with my thumb and forefinger. "Here's the message:

"'Dear Mrs. Moreau:
Saying that I'm sorry about everything is so appallingly

inadequate that it seems ludicrous. But I'll say it anyway—I am sorry. I know how you felt about him, and I
also know how much he cared for you.

> Good-bye,
> Gretchen Frazier' "

"That's all there is?" Cramer said, breaking the
silence in the room.

"That's it," I answered. "What were you expecting—a
signed and notarized confession with three witnesses?"

"I want to see that letter," Hobson gruffed. "When
did you get it, Mrs. Moreau? And why weren't we told
about it?"

Elena twisted in her chair to face the back of the
room. "It was in my departmental box this afternoon and
I only got around to looking at it while I was having
dinner at home just before we left to come here."

"Were you and this Frazier girl good friends?"
Cramer demanded.

"No. I'd only met her two or three times, although I
knew she and Hale were . . . close. I doubt if we'd
spoken more than a few sentences to each other."

"Is this her writing?" Hobson grabbed the letter
from me. When he checked later, those fingerprints on it
other than Gretchen's would be his, plus one smudged
print from Elena.

"I don't know," Elena said, shaking her head. "I
assume so, but I just don't know." A tear rolled down her
cheek.

"Mr. Hobson, it will be simple enough to determine
the handwriting," Wolfe said, averting his eyes from the
sobbing woman. "If you happen to be a betting man and
doubt that Gretchen Frazier was the author of that
missive, I suggest that you might wish to propose a wager
to Mr. Goodwin, who enjoys such things."

Hobson looked like he wanted to either pop Wolfe or
cut loose with a string of those words that can't be used on
television. But bless him, he showed admirable restraint
by gritting his teeth, getting up, and storming out of the
office. Lieutenant Powers, looking just as grim, was right

on his heels, and I was only too happy to follow them both down the hall and hold the front door open. After all, in the brownstone we have certain standards where the social graces are concerned.

TWENTY-THREE

The wall clock read eleven-sixteen. Wolfe and I were alone in the office, nursing beer and milk, respectively. After our guests had filed out, I helped Fritz straighten up, putting chairs back where they belonged, taking glasses to the kitchen, and otherwise giving the place a semipresentable look that Fritz would improve upon in the morning.

"Well, you managed to make just about everybody unhappy tonight," I told Wolfe.

"Oh?" He set his beer glass down and raised his eyebrows.

"Sure. First there's our client, who paid up all right, which is the good news," I said, holding the check for twenty-five thousand dollars that Cortland had somewhat grudgingly written as his second and final installment just before he left. "But he's sore at you because you made his hero look like a dirty old man—which of course he was. Then there's Prescott's top cop, who's mad because you solved his case for him and didn't even leave him anybody to arrest. To say nothing of Cramer and Stebbins, who probably felt like they wasted their evening. You know how Purley likes to give his handcuffs a workout. And we have Schmidt and Greenbaum, the Frick and Frack of the Prescott faculty, who were hoping Markham had either committed suicide or fallen accidentally. Now they're afraid that despite his lecherous leanings he'll look like a martyr and will end up being deified. And I've still got to call Lon, who's sure to be grouchy because he won't get the kind of story he was hoping for. After all, the headline PRIVATE GUMSHOE SAYS PRESCOTT COED KILLED PROF THEN SELF BUT POLICE ARE SEEKING PROOF isn't exactly a newsstand grabber. He was expecting you to finger somebody who's living so the *Gazette* could somehow wangle an exclusive interview with the suspect. As for Elena, she had to sit there and listen while you speculated on the amorous exploits of the man she felt she had some claim on."

"Mr. Markham's exploits, as you refer to them, surely came as no surprise to her," Wolfe remarked.

"I know. Still, it's got to be hard hearing about them, especially in front of a crowd that includes some of your coworkers. But you sent at least one person home happy—Potter. Now that there's nothing stopping him from latching on to that dough of Bach's, he's free to keep on building his empire up the Hudson. No doubt Prescott will have a Bach Library, a Bach Field House, and a Bach Science Center before it's over.

"There's one thing that still puzzles me, though," I said. "You'd be the first one to admit you're not much for reading fiction; how in hell did you know that all three of those books on Markham's list had something to do with May-and-September romances?"

The folds in Wolfe's cheeks deepened. "I was wondering when that would occur to you," he said, pouring beer and watching the foam settle. "While you are correct that my reading tastes run to nonfiction, you know that I make it a point to read *about* books. In one source or another, I probably have read reviews of ten thousand novels over the years, including of the three titles to which you refer. And as you also know, I *remember* what I read."

Okay, that sounds like bragging—and it is. But as far as I'm concerned, he can brag like that every time he fills our coffers with fifty thousand simoleons.

TWENTY-FOUR

I was right about Lon, of course. He'd been counting on a living, breathing culprit, but nonetheless he made do and whipped together a colorful story, complete with quotes from Wolfe, Hobson, and Potter ("I'm just glad this horror is behind us and that we at Prescott can turn our attention back toward our mission as educators."). Wolfe's picture got in, too, although mine didn't make it. "Space considerations" was how Lon explained it to me later.

The handwriting on the note to Elena checked out as Gretchen Frazier's, of course, and based on this plus further investigation that included a lengthy phone conversation with Wolfe, the Orange County medical examiner up in Goshen amended the death certificates to read homicide for Markham and death by manner of suicide for Gretchen.

The *Gazette* and the other New York dailies had another piece on Prescott a few months later. They each covered a press conference on the campus in which plans were unveiled for the hundred million dollar Leander Bach Center for Science and Technology, a "state-of-the-art complex" for which ground would be broken sometime in the spring. They all carried the same photo—Potter and Bach grinning and standing on either side of an easel with an architect's rendering of the buildings.

And oh, yes—I finally did get my long October weekend with Lily at her hideaway in Dutchess County, where we had three wonderful days doing as much of nothing as possible. On Monday, when I asked if she wanted to ride back to the city with me in the Mercedes, she said thanks anyway, but she wasn't quite ready to trade the fall colors for the concrete and carbon monoxide just yet.

That meant I was alone driving south, with the option of detouring across the river to Prescott on the chance that a certain auburn-haired receptionist might be free for lunch.

I did, and she was.